I0728026

Stone Shadow:

A Paranormal Protector Tale

Book 4 in the Heart of Steel series

DEMELZA CARLTON

This book was created with the assistance of a grant from the Western Australian Department of Local Government, Sport and Cultural Industries.

Copyright © 2023 Demelza Carlton

Lost Plot Press

All rights reserved.

ONE

"Woo woo! Woo woo!" sang Callie and Tacey in the back seat of the car, too drunk to remember the rest of the words of the Rolling Stones song they'd insisted on listening to all the way home.

Octavia just shook her head. From the quiet of a mining camp to summoning demons and then driving her drunk family home…her life was crazier than she'd ever believed it could be when she'd live at home with her parents. And she wouldn't trade it for the world - not even listening to Callie and Tacey's off key singing. Damn, she'd missed the girls while she was up north.

Though where they'd come up with the idea of trying to summon demons in a cemetery of all places, Octavia had no idea. Evidently she'd been gone too long if they were planning crazy stuff like this.

Not that any of them actually believed they'd be able to summon a demon. Even Callie with her library of old spell books didn't believe in magic, as she told everyone who'd listen, several times a day.

Good thing, too. If they'd summoned a demon, and it had heard this song, the poor bugger probably would have fled right back to hell, covering its ears as it went.

She had to laugh. Fortunately for Callie and Tacey, they both had other talents that didn't require them to make a living from their musical abilities. Not that Octavia was much better, but she wasn't the one singing her lungs out the window on the freeway.

"Can you close the windows? It's cold," Octavia said.

She had to repeat the request a few times before either of the girls heard her, before they began fumbling with the winding mechanism.

Next car, she was going to get power windows in the back seat.

When she could afford another car…

Octavia sighed. Well, that wouldn't be this week. Besides, this one still drove okay. It had gotten them to the graveyard, and it would get them home.

In the rear view mirror, she glimpsed a winged shadow flying behind them for a moment, before it vanished. Big bird to be out at night. She wasn't sure how big an owl's wingspan was, but that one looked big enough to take on a wedge tailed eagle.

Or maybe it had been a swan or something, gliding down to the river to sleep.

Tacey had found a different song to sing, and Octavia actually knew the words to this one, so she joined them for a bit. Why the hell not? It was girls' night, after all, and they hadn't been out for a long time, thanks to this bloody pandemic.

Pity there weren't antivirus programs for people viruses the way there were for computers. If there were, she'd have hit this virus so hard, people would have already forgotten it had ever existed by now.

But tonight, with the girls, she could forget. No constant testing like at the mine site, or at the airport. She was home now, and her time was her own. Or, in this case, Tacey's and Callie's, and she didn't begrudge them a minute of it.

She bumped down the driveway, taking the curves slowly, as it had been a few weeks since she'd driven them in the dark. Then the girls were stumbling out of the car, and they probably would have ended up sleeping on the veranda if she hadn't been there to unlock the door for them.

"You're the best sister ever. Dunno what I'd

do without you," Tacey slurred, planting a big, smacking kiss on each of Octavia's cheeks before she stumbled off to bed.

Octavia just shook her head. Tacey would do just fine without her – she always did. A single mum, a café owner, and the unchallenged leader of their little household, there was nothing Tacey couldn't do. If Octavia hadn't been home, Tacey would have been the designated driver, and she'd probably have done an even better job. That was just…Tacey. And Octavia was lucky to have her.

If it wasn't for Tacey, Octavia might still be living at home, hedged around by all her parents' rules, instead of free to live her life as a responsible adult. Well, semi-responsible. She was only responsible for herself, after all, and no one noticed if she stayed up all night and had chocolate for breakfast. Except Rory, Tacey's daughter, who was having a sleepover with her grandparents tonight, or Tacey would never have touched the vodka.

Callie's door slammed and Octavia heard the creak of Tacey climbing into bed. She'd done her bit and gotten them safely home.

Now…maybe she could sneak out and get some work done.

TWO

If dying on one of his brother's stupid schemes wasn't bad enough, waking up in a god damned graveyard was worse. No, waking up with his brother and his two stupid cousins, who'd agreed to the scheme in the first place. Not for the first time, Harlow wished he'd stayed in Scotland.

But here he at least had a farm of his own. Or he would have, if his brother's stupidity hadn't cost him that, too.

Help.

He arrowed toward the call, just as he'd run toward Grant when the idiot got himself shot, only to realise it wasn't Grant's voice this time, but a woman's.

Wasn't a woman the reason they'd gotten into this mess?

And the others appeared ready to fight over her like animals.

Harlow's breath hissed out between his teeth. There was more than one voice calling for help, therefore there was more than one woman. Four women, and four of them.

Of course, he'd have to be the only voice of reason this time, too. Stan had already claimed the girl at his feet, which left three. The redhead went to Wystan, in memory of the wife he'd lost. The witch who'd summoned them, her call the clearest of all, and likely more trouble than the rest put together, would be Grant's responsibility. Which left him to help the one driving the tiny horseless carriage two of the girls had crowded into. A strange conveyance to his eyes, though the roads were full of similar ones.

How much time had passed for trains to take over from horses and carriages? These looked very different from the locomotive he'd once seen in Glasgow. No smoke, for a start. And if a slip of a girl could drive one…

When the others seemed set on following the women into the house, Harlow stopped them. "Gargoyles go on the roof, not inside a lady's bedchamber!" he snapped.

Wystan had landed beside him, appreciating the wisdom of maintaining his distance.

Grant just smirked and said, "You do what you wish. I will answer my lady's call, no matter what she asks of me," before vanishing into the house.

Harlow waited and waited, but the fool did not return. Likely the witch had cast some sort of curse on him. A curse he richly deserved, no doubt.

Harlow considered entering the house to

save him, as he'd done a thousand times before. Grant would get into scrapes, and Harlow would always get him out again.

Not this time. After getting himself and Harlow killed, Grant was on his own. He could save himself, if he was capable of such a thing.

"Aren't you going to go after him?" Wystan asked, as though reading Harlow's mind.

Harlow could never be sure how much Wystan perceived. Half the time, he seemed to still be mourning his wife, but sometimes…sometimes he seemed like the level-headed man Harlow had once known, before love had addled his brain.

Harlow drew in a deep breath. He'd promised his parents he'd watch over Grant, especially in this dangerous land of Western Australia, so far from home. But his parents were long dead. Hell, he and Grant had been long dead, brought back to life only by his witch's spell. Death negated all oaths, even promises exacted on one's deathbed. He was free of his promises. Free to follow the girl in the horseless carriage as she drove it away from the house, into the darkness.

Harlow spread his wings. "No. I must protect her. A woman driving in the dark could be beset by all kinds of dangers." One flap, then another, and he soared off after her.

THREE

Everything in the studio above the café looked exactly like she'd left it, before Octavia headed north. Well, almost exactly. The bed linen looked freshly washed, and Rochelle had made the bed way more neatly than Octavia ever did. All the coffee cups that usually sat on the desk were gone, too, and the rings wiped away. The joys of working above a café owned by her sister – she had a never ending supply of good coffee, even in the middle of the night, and a proper espresso machine to make it with, any time she wanted.

Anything was better than the instant stuff she'd had to endure in the mining camp.

With great care, as it had been several weeks since she'd last made a decent coffee, Octavia brewed herself a mocha, then carried it upstairs. Her computer had finished updating, so she clicked open the 3D rendering program and surveyed her progress on the pilot. Not bad, actually. The people looked realistic enough, but the vegetation could do with some work. And the lighting…it just wasn't quite right. In 1829, they'd had sunlight and firelight. That was it. It had to look real, so when you put on the headset and stepped into the world, it was like you were standing in the Swan River Colony, instead of a simulation. Nothing less would do. This was about her family's history, the women who'd gone against the odds to survive and raise children who'd become her ancestors. Left a legacy like Tacey would.

Thinking of all the women who'd come before her, whose stories hadn't been told by the men who'd put their names to roads and monuments, harbours and history books, who were the real heroes of that time, Octavia took a deep breath. Then she sent a call to the universe, to help her bring their stories to light.

FOUR

Every second well-lit sign proclaimed that this was Fremantle, but the town of tents and converted horse boxes had come a long way from the place Harlow remembered. The Round House on Arthur Head had witnessed it all, for it still stood, looking more like a fort than the prison it had once been. Even the brothels on Bannister Street were gone, though the taverns remained. No longer tents, they'd gained walls and become stately hotels with balconies lining South Terrace. This shining town would put soot-smeared Glasgow to shame.

Harlow was quite happy admiring the place from his eyrie atop of the roof of the building his charge had entered. When she'd left her vehicle and dared to walk the dark street alone, he'd worried for her welfare, but she'd reached the building without mishap, and locked the door behind her, before climbing the stairs to the small apartment he'd glimpsed above the shop.

The lights within her apartment were as bright as those outside, and they gave off less smoke than even the finest whale oil. This was a remarkable time to be alive.

Help.

Without the other girls' voices to drown her out, he heard her call clearly. A rich, husky voice he had not expected from someone who looked so young. Nor did he expect her commanding tone — as though she fully expected him to respond.

He found himself moving from the roof to her side, before he'd even thought about responding, such was her pull.

Had he been mistaken in sending Grant after the witch, when this woman seemed even more powerful?

Harlow closed his eyes. He would simply be properly respectful, so as not to arouse her ire, and all would be well. He would answer her call, fulfil whatever task she required, and he'd be up on the roof, admiring the view again in next to no time.

Harlow stepped out of the wall, dropping to one knee like she was the Queen.

She didn't say a word.

He dared to glance up. She had her back to him, her gaze fixed on a sort of glowing tablet before her. Harlow squinted at it. By all that was holy – it was like she'd read his mind. On the tablet was an almost perfect picture of Fremantle as he remembered it, right down to the brackish swamp where this building now stood.

He coughed, then bowed his head as she started to turn around.

"Harlow Steel, at your service, my lady," he said.

A sharp intake of breath. "How did you get in here?"

"I arrived on the sailing ship *Hooghly*, under the command of Captain Peter Reeves, though we almost came to grief on the rocks outside the harbour. But that is immaterial. I am here at your service. You called for help, and I am here to answer your call." He dared to raise his head, to find her curious gaze fixed on him.

There wasn't an ounce of fear in her expression. "Are you Rochelle and Tacey's Moth Man? I have to admit, you look more like a gargoyle than a giant moth to me. Horns instead of antennae, and the rock hard sculpted muscles. I thought moths were more…fluffy. Well, whatever you are, those wings are amazing, not to mention the full body makeup. It all looks real."

"I am indeed real, and at your service. What is your wish, my lady?"

"It's Octavia, not anyone's lady, and I'm afraid I don't need special effects makeup, even as good as yours right now. What I'm in need of is an expert in early colonial construction and farming practices in 1820s and 30s Fremantle."

Harlow couldn't hide his smile. "Then I am indeed at your service, Lady Octavia. If I may be so bold, you have painted a remarkable likeness of the Swan River Settlement there." He rose to his feet. "May I approach to admire the painting more closely?"

She frowned. "Oh, the paintings were the work of Mary Ann Friend and Jane Eliza Currie. 1830 and 1831, respectively, as evidenced by – "

"The Round House on Arthur Head and the proliferation of limestone construction, among other things," Harlow finished for her. "In 1830, there were only a handful of huts and horse boxes among the canvas city."

"Yes." She stared at him in wonder. "How have I never seen you at the university? The archaeology department isn't that big…"

Not just a lady, but a lady scholar, and a lovely one at that. A woman worthy of protection, for certain.

"I'm no scholar, Lady Octavia. I just know my history."

"Pull up a chair, then. I'd value your opinion."

Hardly daring to believe his good luck, Harlow swore he'd serve Lady Octavia for as long as she'd have him, Grant and the rest of those idiots be damned.

FIVE

"See, while Fremantle is interesting and all, what I really wish I knew more about is Clarence Town, the place Thomas Peel's group settlement scheme landed and lived until he was allocated land to replace his original land grant. There are plenty of paintings and sketches of Fremantle, but Clarence Town…there's a couple of written accounts, usually from outsiders who didn't live there, some history books that put it at Woodman Point, which are definitely wrong, and then there are the archaeology investigation reports. Now, those reports support some of the accounts – like the fires and where the buildings were – but there's so little left, because people lived there for such a short time. Only a year or so, before they all dispersed. Whereas Fremantle just grew and grew until it became…well, this." Octavia waved her hand in the air.

"Well, the first thing you must know is only Thomas Peel and outsiders from the Governor's office called it Clarence Town. The passengers who sailed on the *Hooghly* called the place Hooghly Town, for there wasn't even a source of fresh water there until the second officer from the ship stumbled across a spring. And sometimes it seemed like there were two towns, really, for the *Hooghly* passengers kept themselves apart from the *Gilmore* people, though they shared both a graveyard and a tavern. And Peel stayed on the beach beside his storehouse, apart from everyone."

He'd definitely done his research. Maybe even more than she had.

"See, that's exactly what I want to know more about. I mean, my many times great grandmother arrived on the *HMS Sulphur* with her brother in 1829. Then five years later, she married a guy who's listed as arriving on the *Hooghly*, though he's not on the passenger list. Maybe he was crew, or someone they picked up at one of the ports along the way…but it's his life that's the mystery, or at least until he married Carline," Octavia said.

Did she imagine it, or did he react to the mention of her many times great grandmother's name? No, she must have imagined it. No one outside the family knew much about Carline. She hadn't featured in any of the history books, unlike her brother, though there were a number of family legends about her. How she'd been a crack shot with a rifle, and how she'd sit on the front steps of Bell Cottage with her favourite rifle across her lap to greet visitors. And the cats. Bell Cottage had always had the best mousers in the entire Swan River Colony, all descended from Salis, the ship's cat she'd adopted. The resident cat at Bell House, which no one had ever fed, yet it presented them with rat and snake corpses nightly, must be one of Salis's descendants. That cat was a mouse murdering machine.

She found Harlow staring at her, his eyebrows raised as if he expected an answer to a question she hadn't heard.

She shook her head. "Sorry, what did you say?"

"Have you seen Clarence Town?" Harlow asked.

"Once," she admitted. "I drove down there to see if I could visualise any of what was in the archaeology reports. But it's just bush. I couldn't even find all of the tracks, and then it started raining, so I headed home." Because once the storm clouds came in over the ocean, there was nothing to stop the rain pelting in sideways in that lonely, unsheltered spot.

"We could head out there now, if you want. I can point out what I know of the place, to give you a better idea of what the camp looked like," he said eagerly.

A sensible girl would refuse, and go home to bed. It was nearly dawn, after all, and she'd been talking to Harlow half the night. Mum would be horrified if she ever knew she'd been talking to a man, alone, up here while the café was closed. If Mum found out she'd gone out in the bush with the same strange man she'd met in the middle of the night...

Octavia grinned. "Sure, why not? It's not dawn yet." She eyed him. Not that the costume wasn't sexy as hell, but... "Don't you want to change into something a bit more practical? I mean, bushwalking in winter won't be kind to your costume."

"I didn't bring any other clothes," Harlow said.

Of course he hadn't. People wanted to see the Moth Man, not a man in ordinary civvies.

Octavia sighed. "Don't tell Tacey, but I did

a couple of photo shoots up here with male models, and I probably still have a couple of the outfits we used for that charity calendar shoot…" She dug through the box of props. A business shirt, a flannel one, an artfully ripped t-shirt…there were plenty of shirts that might fit him, but she hadn't bothered to buy many pants. Actually, the only pair of pants were black tracksuit bottoms, with a grey stripe running up the side. She couldn't even remember using these in the shoot. Oh, wait, for that guy who posed as a fighter, with the pants slung so low on his hips, she'd had to tape them in place. By the time she'd cropped the shot for the calendar, the final version hadn't even shown the pants in the picture.

While Harlow got changed in the bathroom downstairs, she set her computer to rendering the pilot version of her world. It would probably take the rest of the night and half the next day, but it would be ready by the time she got back tomorrow night.

She heard footsteps thundering back up the

stairs.

She hadn't thought track pants could possibly look hot on a guy then, and now…well, Harlow could keep them. He looked better than the model.

"I'm ready," he said, folding his wings behind him.

Well, if that's what he wanted to wear…

"Let's go, then," she said.

SIX

"Where's your car?" Octavia asked as she locked the door to the café.

It took Harlow a moment to realise she was referring to a horseless carriage. She must have been born a fine lady indeed, to not realise most men could not afford to keep a horse, let alone a carriage. Or were things different in this time?

He stretched his wings. "I'd prefer to fly."

He could enjoy the view while he flew behind her car, perhaps even glimpse the lay of the land before they arrived so he could lead her to the shack he and the others had shared for that first tumultuous year on the Indian Ocean shore. A year that was now almost centuries in the past, he'd learned in his conversation with Octavia, along with her distaste for titles, be they Lady or even just Miss.

"But what would your mother say if she knew you'd allowed a man you'd just met to call you by your first name?" he'd said.

Only to be greeted by the most enchanting, yet mischievous grin he'd ever beheld. Without an ounce of guilt, she'd merely shrugged and said, "Better than shortening it. If anyone calls me anything but the full four syllables of Octavia, she goes nuclear. Mum probably thinks the sacrosanctity of Augustus's sister extends to any woman called Octavia. At least Tacey got a nickname, if only because I couldn't say her name properly as a kid."

So many times during the conversation,

she'd looked at him the same way she did now – calculating and thoughtful, like she was weighing his words with far more care than he'd used when he uttered them, so that she might respond appropriately.

This time, she said, "You're not flying. Get in."

She'd had to help him fasten the seatbelt she insisted he wear, after he'd snagged it on his wings. Her capable hands on his bare skin did not hesitate, nor shy away. Few women of his own time would have been so bold, and he had to admit he liked it.

He'd watched her drive from the air earlier, but sitting beside her, he was struck again with how expertly she handled the vehicle. This woman had no need for anyone's help, least of all his, yet she'd called for it twice.

Then again, if she chose to keep him by her side, she also kept him out of whatever trouble Grant and the others would get him into if he stayed near them. Harlow had no complaints.

Octavia drew the car to a halt in a large

open area that could have been a coaching yard, if there were any coaches or horses to be seen. Then Harlow stepped out of the vehicle, and saw where they were. His breath caught in his throat.

The sound of the waves on the beach below the cliffs dragged him back two centuries. Even in the dim light, he fancied the buildings between him and the beach were Peel's cottage and his storehouses. Harlow half expected the man to come stomping out to berate him for bringing another useless mouth to feed into a community that could ill afford it.

But there would have been no space for Octavia in the shack he shared with his brother and his cousins. For her, he'd have to build a cottage with a loft, and a proper hearth, beneath a roof that didn't leak when the rain came down. Somewhere with a better water supply, that wasn't befouled with so many people living too close together. Somewhere women didn't die in squalor, to be buried in the dip between the sand dunes where he and the other single men had dug far too many graves for such a small community.

With the water at his back, Harlow moved instinctively to where he knew the track was, or where it had been, the one that led from Peel's house to his own. Scrub had grown up, forcing him to take a roundabout path instead of a direct one, but he'd know these hills any day, for he'd walked them every day for a year. The track opened up, for someone had seen fit to pave it during the intervening years, though they'd also moved it north, too, so the cemetery was on the south side of the track instead of off to the north. Before, you'd have to take a side track to reach the cemetery, hidden from sight so that they weren't reminded that death was their constant companion in this dangerous new land.

Now, the track cut over the ridge behind it, so Harlow could peer down at the graves of those laid to rest so long ago. No markers remained to tell him who lay buried beneath the sand, but it seemed only yesterday he'd lifted the cold, limp bodies from the dead house into their final resting place. Gentle souls who hadn't possessed the rough strength to endure such conditions…along with brave souls who'd given everything they had so that their families would survive, only to fall before they could see the future they'd bought for them.

Harlow dropped into the graveyard, falling to his knees. He'd pay his respects first, before venturing up the hill to his own place in this chaos that had come from Peel's ill-fated settlement scheme.

After two hundred years, did anything more than bones remain? A ghost, or maybe something like him? Harlow lowered his forehead to the sand, sending out whatever strange, gargoyle sense that allowed him to seek out danger.

There was a faint…something…

But the sun chose that moment to rise above the ridge, caressing Harlow with its relentless rays, and he turned to unyielding, unfeeling stone.

SEVEN

The moment the car stopped, Harlow took off into the scrub, his long legs and relentless strides taking him out of sight in a moment before Octavia had even managed to take her seatbelt off.

She shouted for him to wait, but it was already too late – he'd disappeared, and she wasn't sure if he could hear her at all.

Swearing, she set off down the track, in the

direction he'd headed. Surely she should see him up ahead soon…

She considered getting out her phone and using the flashlight function, but the sky was already lightening with the approaching dawn, and any moment now, it would rise in the east and blind her.

"Harlow, where are you?" she shouted.

No answer.

She made it all the way up to the Mount Brown lookout, calling every few minutes, but even from that high point, she couldn't see him. He'd vanished into thin air.

If he hadn't been a ghost she'd imagined in the first place.

She wasn't sure whether to laugh or cry at that thought.

He'd been so knowledgeable about the early colony – more than anyone she'd ever met, except for some of the academics at uni. She couldn't have conjured up a more helpful hallucination. Where her subconscious had gotten the idea for the horns and wings, though, or the muscles…maybe that had come from the demon summoning ritual at the cemetery with the other girls. Yes, that would be her excuse and she was sticking to it.

Well, you knew it was time for bed if the sun was up, and your helpful demon ghost hallucination had disappeared with the dawn. Maybe Callie's spell had worked and they had summoned something after all, though not what they'd been aiming for. Instead of a protector for Alethea, she'd gotten a know-it-all history buff for a night.

Was it wrong to wish to have him for one more night? Harlow had definitely been hotter than any of her professors or tutors…

Shaking her head, Octavia headed back to the car. She called Harlow's name a few times, halfheartedly, but he still didn't appear, so she climbed back into the car and drove home.

EIGHT

"Eeee!" Rory's otherworldly screech was way too loud to have come from such a small person. "Don't let it touch me!"

Tacey sounded much more reasonable. "It's just a cricket. It won't hurt you."

"But it might jump on me!"

"Okay, I'll just go get the bug spray…"

"No! You can't kill it! You have to catch bugs and put them outside, Mrs K said. It's better for the environment!"

For a six-year-old who adored a show about a bounty hunter, she sure didn't like killing things.

"Okay…so, if I can get it to hop into this cup…"

Aww, Tacey was the sweetest mum. Their own mother would have used the spray and flushed the corpse down the loo by now, but between the sounds of the plastic cup hitting various surfaces and Rory's cries of, "Get it! Catch it, Mummy! Oh, you missed! Catch it!" it sounded like they were going to save the bug's life whether it wanted to be saved or not. Just as long as the cat didn't see it – one crunch and it'd be dead.

Maybe Octavia should help…

The trill of Tacey's phone drew Octavia to the kitchen instead.

The caller ID said it was Bruce from the backpackers.

Octavia's blood ran cold. The backpackers next to the café? Shit, if something bad had happened to the café, it would break Tacey. So she answered the call.

"Hello?"

"Hi, this is Bruce. I manage the backpackers next door to the Shut Up Café. One of the guys staying here heard glass breaking, but it wasn't here, and I saw the café door open, even though it's closed, so I called the police and they're over there now and…"

"I'll be right there. Thanks, Bruce," Octavia said, snatching up her car keys.

She considered telling Tacey, but there was no way she'd hear over Rory's shrieks, and Octavia could handle this. She prayed that the universe would somehow help her handle this.

She sped all the way to the café, and considered it a miracle that the first police she saw were the ones standing on the footpath outside.

"What's happened?" Octavia asked.

One of the police officers frowned. "Are you Tac…Tac…Miss Bell?"

"I am Miss Bell, but not Tacita," Octavia

said, pronouncing her sister's name slowly in the hope they might remember it. "I'm Octavia, the other sister." And the other name on the lease, for when stuff like this happened and Tacey was too busy being mum of the year to deal with it.

They both looked relieved. "Did you leave the door open?"

"No, we always lock the café up for the night when we close. The manager from next door called me and said he heard breaking glass, but the door looks okay..." Octavia swallowed. There was a lot of glass inside. "Is it safe to go in?"

"With your permission, we can check for you."

Permission she was only too happy to give. She followed them in, though, not happy to stay outside. If there was damage, she needed to see it. Then sort it, before Tacey saw it.

At first, the café looked fine.

"Any idea where this came from?" one officer asked, pointing at the floor behind the counter.

Octavia took a deep breath, and stepped forward. There was glass everywhere, a whole carpet of shards and slivers so small, she'd have to vacuum it up to be sure she got it all.

The counter looked intact, though, along with all the glassware stacked along the wall. It took Octavia a long moment to realise the glass cabinet that sat on top of the counter beside the cash register, usually full of whatever pastries, cakes or muffins Tacey had made for the day, was missing.

"The cake cabinet, I guess," Octavia said. She tried to describe the size and shape with her hands. "It usually sits here, but it was really heavy. It took two of us to lift it, the last time we had to clean under it."

"Someone really hated that cabinet, then. A disgruntled customer, maybe?"

Octavia could only shake her head. "Everyone liked Tacey's muffins. Everybody. Even her gluten free ones were amazing, and actually gluten free, not like other places I could name. I don't know how it could be in so many pieces. I mean, even if you dropped it down the stairs and jumped up and down on it, you wouldn't be able to…" Octavia swallowed.

"What about if you bashed it with a brick?" the officer asked, nudging something half hidden beneath the counter with his foot. Sure enough, it was a brick – or half of one. It looked like it had come from the courtyard behind the backpackers, which also ran behind their building.

"I guess…" She couldn't imagine wanting to do something like that. Or anyone wanting to smash something of Tacey's. It was just…unimaginable. "Maybe they were angry that there was no money in the till, so they took it out on the nearest thing." She'd seen some of the guys up north at mine sites do crazy shit like that. On drugs, some of them, even with routine drug testing that was supposed to stop that, plus some of those guys had issues that went way beyond the need for anger management. There were whispers of criminal records and time in prison for violent crimes, but no one could ever actually confirm it, and she'd never wanted to hack into the personnel records to find out. Not that it took much hacking, when you managed all the IT systems, including the HR ones, but…there were some things you just didn't want to know. It was better to believe the best, as opposed to the worst of people.

The police officer didn't look like he believed it, but he didn't say so. Just kept going toward the kitchen.

The kitchen and the store room were untouched. Whoever had come in hadn't wanted food or cooking equipment.

"Looks like this is where they got in," said a voice from upstairs.

Where Octavia kept all her best equipment…

She raced up the stairs, two at a time, almost dizzy from holding her breath by the time she got to the top. She released her breath in a relieved hiss when she saw her computer was still there, and the storage box that held her camera equipment was still covered by the cloth that made it look like nothing more than a coffee table.

Yes, everything was still there, exactly as she'd left it before she headed north. The only sign that anyone had been here was the glass on the floor from the broken window. These shards were bigger, not smashed to powder like the cabinet downstairs.

The police officer leaned out the window. "Yep, it looks like they climbed up the drainpipe, then bent it over to the window so they could use it to climb in." He tapped on the floor. "Left some water here, too. You'll need to mop that up before it damages the floor boards, or leaks through the ceiling below."

"Don't you need to dust for fingerprints or something first?" Octavia said. Yes, cleaning up was important, but even more important was catching whoever had done this so it wouldn't happen again.

"Is there anyone who might have reasons to want to hurt you or your sister?" the officer asked.

"Only her ex, but he's in prison for trying to kill her," Octavia said. "He's not likely to be climbing drainpipes and smashing cabinets for quite a few years yet." Forever, if she had her way. The justice system had been way too lenient with Matt, probably because he was a white boy who went to a fancy private school. If he'd been anyone else… "Probably some drug addict looking for cash. I've seen other business owners put the empty cash drawer in the window when they close at night, so burglars know not to bother. Maybe we should try that." She tapped her foot impatiently, then winced at the crunch of glass under her shoe. "Can I start cleaning up now?"

"Just need to check for prints," the other officer said as he lumbered up the stairs.

It took another half hour before they were done, and she was allowed to lock the door behind them. Only then did she dig out the massive industrial vacuum cleaner to start on the café floor.

She filled it up twice and had to empty it into the dumpster out the back and she'd barely made a dent in the mess. At this rate, she'd be cleaning all night.

"Can I help with anything?"

Octavia dropped the vacuum hose in surprise.

Harlow stood beside the counter, wearing nothing but his borrowed track pants from yesterday, Looking for all the world like nothing had happened.

She grabbed his arm and squeezed. He felt real enough, and not at all like a hallucination. Then again, if she was hallucinating, it wouldn't be so much a stretch from seeing and hearing Harlow to thinking she could feel him, too.

"What happened last night? Where did you go?" she demanded.

He hung his head. "I'm sorry about that. I

meant to take you to Hooghly Town, but I got distracted by the cemetery, and then the sun came up and I was stuck."

"Stuck."

"It's a gargoyle thing. When we're exposed to direct sunlight, we turn to stone, like a statue on a roof. We can't move or speak again until we're out of the sun, or the sun goes down."

So now she wasn't just imagining a guy in a gargoyle suit, but an actual gargoyle? She'd been reading too many of Callie's monster romances.

"Right…"

"We can go again once we're finished with…whatever you need my help with here, if you want," he said.

"After I'm done cleaning up here, I'm going home to get some sleep. I probably need it, if I'm calling up monsters from my subconscious to help with the cleaning. I would have thought woodland creatures would be more…appropriate…" Octavia had to suppress a snort. Woodland creatures only worked for princesses, and Rory was adamant that none of them were princesses. She evidently hadn't watched *The Princess and the Frog* yet, then. Maybe on the weekend…

"What can I do to help?" Harlow asked.

A man volunteering to do cleaning. That wasn't an offer Octavia was about to turn down, hallucination or not. "Well, if you could start dealing with the broken glass upstairs while I finish up here, then I can come up and mop the floor. Uh, and I need to find something to board the window up with, until I can get someone out to repair it."

"Yes, ma'am." Harlow headed upstairs.

Of course she'd hallucinated a man whose arse looked amazing in track pants.

Octavia shook her head, and got back to work.

NINE

When the sun finally set, Harlow had headed back to the house to offer his apologies to Octavia for deserting her, and not answering her calls, only to find that she wasn't home. Worse, Grant and Wystan had taken up residence on the roof, like big ugly cockerels, so he'd darted into the walls of the ruined cottage further down the hill to wait for Octavia's return.

She'd been busy with her family in the house for several hours, so he'd waited, distracted by the small ginger cat hunting rats in the palm trees. He'd never seen such an efficient killer. One, two, three, four…the cat soon had a row of corpses laid out before the front steps of the cottage, and she showed no signs of slowing the carnage.

Help me.

Harlow could not resist the siren call of Octavia's voice, but he didn't want to, either. Only this time, she sped off in her car without him, leaving him to follow the red glow of her rear lights from the air.

She headed for the café where they'd first met last night, only she wasn't alone. Two police officers were present, investigating what appeared to be a break in at the café.

Harlow slipped between the walls, watching and listening. The police believed the attack was personal, while Octavia seemed to think the motive was merely theft. Reducing glass to powder, though…that took effort, even for a man with stone fists. For a normal man…that kind of damage took a fair amount of rage. And if someone who would do that to a cabinet was after Octavia, Harlow would protect her, no matter what. Let the bastard fight a man his own size, instead of preying on helpless women. Or even capable women.

Finally, the police left, and Harlow dared to step out into the café where Octavia could see him.

"Can I help with anything?" he asked. She had asked for help, after all, and in the absence of an attacker to pummel, he might as well be of some use.

She sent him upstairs, where he'd seen more glass from the broken window. Picking up the pieces was easy, for glass was no match for his living stone skin, but finding something to mend the window took longer. He found a packing crate that was about the right size, and proceeded to take it apart, before putting it back together again in a shutter the same size as the window. He'd just finished nailing it in place when Octavia came up the stairs, carrying a mop and bucket.

"Wow," was all she said.

"Where would you like me to put this?" he asked, holding out the bucket of broken glass he'd collected.

She grabbed it out of his hands. "I'll take that. You finish what you were doing with the window."

He was indeed finished by the time she returned, so he'd started mopping the floor.

"You don't need to..." she began. Then she sighed. "I want to believe you're real, but all this is too perfect. You have to be a hallucination, because only an imaginary man could possibly..." She waved her hand up and down, trying to convey something she didn't have the words for.

"I assure you, I am real, and far from perfect, ma'am," Harlow said, dropping the mop into the bucket for the last time. "I still feel guilty for how I left you last night. I've been trying to work out how I might make it up to you. If there's anything you wish of me, you have only to name it, and it shall be done. I swear it."

She wagged a finger at him. "See? Too perfect. I'm probably imagining the way you boarded up the window, too, so I should get a glazier out here first thing to fix the window properly. Good thing I know one who owes me a favour…"

She pulled out a small device, the size of a calling card, and held it to her ear. After speaking into it for a few minutes, she returned it to her pocket. "Right. Repairs sorted. Now, I need to get home, because I just remembered I promised Tacey I'd stay home with Rory while she does the grocery shopping, or I'll have to go to the supermarket, and I never seem to get the right things. And whatever Tacey cooks always tastes better anyway." She pointed a finger at Harlow. "As for you, my perfect hallucination, you can stay here until tomorrow night, when I'll come back to work on my virtual Swan River Colony. Then you can tell me everything you know so I can make it even better than it already is."

Harlow bowed. "I would be honoured."

TEN

It was a rare day when Octavia was awake before lunchtime, especially as she usually went to bed just before dawn, but the morning after the break in was one of them. Everyone else had already left for work and school, so she could totally have spent the day watching TV in her pyjamas, but she was too restless to just lie on the couch. When she'd lived at home, she'd have gone for a run, but now she wanted to direct her energy into something more practical than pounding the pavement.

So she headed to the café, waving hello to Rochelle as she headed upstairs to work on the immersive project. She'd forgotten to check last night if it had finished rendering, and she needed to see the final result before she sent it to the Bicentennial Council with her project application. If they accepted it, she'd have the funding and time to take it from a concept into a full-blown virtual world, which would have its own place in the new WA Museum when it opened at the end of the year.

Then everyone would know Carline's story, among a number of other women who'd worked hard to turn the fledgeling colony into a thriving state with industry that funded most of the country, something people on the east coast had no idea about, either.

Maybe then Mum would believe that the women in their family were more like Carline and Tacey, brave rebels who didn't spend all their time trying to slot into the perfect niche.

No, Bell women broke down walls, blazed trails, and had the courage to not only write their own destinies, but provide for later generations, too.

Bell House was the perfect example. Built to replace the crumbling Bell Cottage that had been Carline's home, it was held in trust as accommodation for Bell women who wanted independence from their family to pursue their own path. Even the lease conditions said no men were allowed to live there – though male children could, as long as their mothers lived in the house. Paying little more than a pittance for rent (because it was a family property, held in trust) had allowed Octavia to keep studying and work on her VR project, when ordinary circumstances would have made her graduate and find a job long before now. Just like Sybil and Alethea. And Tacey…well, Tacey had needed this place as much for herself as she had for Rory. It had given her a place to stay, with a support network of family who could help her with Rory and the café when she needed it, while she'd become a sort of surrogate mum to all of them.

Tacey made sure the bills were paid on time, and that there was food in the fridge. She'd even been known to do a load of laundry for you, if you left it beside the machine or on the line and forgot about it.

So Octavia had to get this project finished, and out there where the public could see just how amazing the Bell women had been over the centuries. It was their legacy, as well as their future. And maybe, just maybe, when she was done telling the stories of women far more amazing than she'd ever be, she'd have the courage to choose a path for herself, something she hadn't even dared to consider until she'd moved into Bell House.

In the years she'd lived in Bell House, she'd considered it, but she still hadn't made any kind of decision. There were so many things she could do with her life…if she only had the courage to do them. If stepping into this finished VR world would give her even a spoonful of the courage her ancestors had possessed, it would be enough.

But the first step was submitted the pilot for funding.

Octavia reached down and flicked on the power switch for her computer.

Nothing.

She pressed it again, harder this time.

Still nothing.

The third time, she held it down like she was trying to do a hard reset on the system. That always got a response – usually an angry beep, followed by the hum of her computer starting up.

Only today…there was still nothing.

A normal person would panic or call IT support.

But Octavia was tech support. At the mine site, they'd called her Batgirl for computers, because obviously she couldn't be Batman. She'd just smiled and thanked them for the compliment. Best that they didn't know the truth…

Only right now, with her tower case wide open and the acrid smell of burned circuitry in the air as she pulled out each dripping, fried piece of what had been functional tech, she felt more like she'd gotten on the wrong side of the Joker.

Water damage she could have dealt with. A big bag of rice and heat would have saved most of her hardware. A bit of burnt wiring would have been regrettable, but replaceable. But this…it was like someone had deliberately poured water through the vents until they'd flooded the machine, and then they'd turned it on, turning the tower into a network of short circuits until the whole mess burned out and fused together into an unsalvageable lump. The only more effective ways to destroy a computer and all the data in it were to use fire or acid.

Whoever had done this knew what they were doing, destroying the computer and all the data on it. Not to mention the graphics card, which had been nearly new and it'd cost her more than the rest of the system combined. You couldn't do proper, immersive virtual reality without a top of the range graphics card, and a system that could handle it.

Octavia's breath hissed out through her teeth. She'd have to start everything from scratch, including building a new system with new hardware. She'd be pushing to meet the grant application deadline with the Bicentennial Council now. Then again, she'd be recreating what she'd already done, and she did have all her notes and the original graphics stored in the cloud. The only thing she didn't have was the render, or the project files she'd used to make the render.

She sighed. She should have let Tacey list the computer system and all her studio equipment on the café's insurance policy, no matter how high the cost. Then she'd have been able to claim the whole replacement system on insurance. But she'd said at the time that it was unlikely anyone would try and steal her cobbled together system, so the price of paying for the extra insurance would be put to better use for equipment upgrades in a year or two.

Upgrades, not a whole new system. Even after working at a mine site, she didn't have enough money to replace the whole system in one hit, and she wouldn't see a cent of that for another week or two.

If she wanted a new computer sooner, she'd have to take on some freelance work in the meantime. The sort of jobs that paid cash on completion.

Oh well. At least she could rejoice in the fact that if her mother knew what she was doing, she'd probably have a conniption. So with a smile on her lips, despite it all, Octavia fished out her laptop and ducked into the dark web to check out the job boards.

ELEVEN

By late afternoon, Octavia calculated she was halfway there. Sure, she could work normal IT support, but it was so much more lucrative when you were fixing problems for people whose businesses were…of questionable legality. It was one thing to fix an ordinary family's printer so their kid could print out an assignment for school, but when a dude who sold fake identification documents downloaded an update that made his computer stop talking to his printer...the support tech who could fix the problem gained superhero status. And a five star review, for service and discretion. Which only earned her even more of a reputation with clients just like him.

So when she needed some ready cash...

Today, she'd fitted a new electronic security system to a motorcycle club's clubhouse, turning the fortress high tech. Admittedly, she'd used a drill more than she'd used her laptop, to fit the electronic locks to all the doors, but even she was impressed by the end of it. And the motorcycle club president was, too, which was why she'd had such a good day.

She'd also done a couple of ordinary tech support call outs, sorting bog-standard computer issues for several cryptocurrency traders. Those she'd been able to do remotely, with a voice synthesiser, which was usually a good thing when dealing with those guys. If they'd known she was a woman...which was why her profile picture was a caricature of a male vampire holding a camera with OTTO emblazoned on a black ribbon underneath. She even gave a discount to anyone who understood the Discworld reference, but she'd only encountered one client who did – a female cryptocurrency trader, as it happened.

She rose from her seat and stretched. She could wait until she had enough for an entire new computer, but she'd learned that the best graphics cards often had to be ordered in, and took longer to arrive than anything else. She had almost enough for the graphics card, so she should probably order that first and leave the rest for the moment.

A quick check of her usual suppliers told her they had no high end graphics cards in stock in right now, no matter which brand she wanted, so she'd be better off calling around tomorrow to see who was expecting an order soonest.

In the meantime, her only other option was the media labs at the university, which she was allowed to access for free while she was still enrolled as a student. They didn't have the best equipment, but it was still better than anything else she'd be able to access for a few weeks. Hopefully, it would be enough to recreate the pilot so she could still apply for the grant...

TWELVE

The mid semester break had started, so the university was almost deserted. It was weird seeing the place so empty in daylight.

The media labs were the exception, though – the place was like a frat house, with boys and their drinks draped across every surface…and every computer.

One of them, a guy who was working on his laptop instead of the dark monitor in front of him, moved aside to let her take his spot. She thanked him and logged on.

For the first time ever, she was glad she used cloud-based software, because the university wasn't silly enough to grant its IT students admin privileges on these machines.

But as she clicked on the file she'd last been working on, all she got was errors. The source files on her old computer were inaccessible, and it would take her hours to swap the links for the backups in the cloud. Then again, it wasn't like she had anything else to do…

Her fingers danced across the keys, replacing link after link. It didn't take long for it to become boring, or for her thoughts to drift away from her task to the conversation going on behind her.

"It has to open with a rap, about how everyone deserted him, but he went it alone anyway."

"I know! We should use *Pirates of Penzance.* Play on that, somehow. Everyone likes that one."

"Can we do that? Isn't that, like, plagiarism and shit?"

"*Hamilton* did it."

"Really?"

"Yep."

Silence reigned for a moment.

Then they all fell over each other to agree that they should absolutely do that, because it had been done in *Hamilton*, which sounded like their holy grail.

Octavia had heard of it, but she'd never seen it. She had seen something about a recording appearing on one of the streaming services, though. Maybe she should make time to watch it. After Rory went to bed, just in case it was something not suitable for kids.

"Ooh, ooh, I got one!" one of the boys said.

It took a minute for the others to fall silent again.

"Yo yo, I'm Thomas Peel

Gonna tell you how my friends and me

Made the Swan River colony real

Want nothing to do with convicts

Cos free is how I feel…"

The boys all clapped, while Octavia fought not to laugh at how awful it was. These boys didn't know the first thing about Peel. The old racist would roll over in his grave if he heard anyone rapping about him. He'd been one of the shooters in the Pinjarra Massacre, for fuck's sake.

"You do know Thomas Peel was a racist rich guy, don't you?" she blurted out.

As one, they turned to glare at her.

One boy drew himself up. "I'm doing my PhD on Peel's life. I think I know him better than you could."

Before Octavia could respond, another kid piped up, "And I'm doing mine on a musical production of the colony's early history. My dad's friends with the Packers, so Crown are already interested in hosting the performance when it's ready."

"We've already applied for a grant from the Bicentennial Council for it, and my dad's on the Council, and he says we're guaranteed approval, especially with all the support we already have," sneered the awful rapper.

Heaven help the little shits. If they ever made it to the stage, the arts community would rip them to shreds.

"Good luck with it, then," she said, logging out of the computer so she could get the fuck out of there.

As if reading her mind, her phone rang and she answered without even looking.

"Is this Otto?"

She hesitated.

The guy on the other end didn't. "Look, the security system you installed isn't working. You better get down here quick, because no one can get into the clubhouse and the president's getting really pissed."

He hung up.

Octavia blew out a breath. Back to the motorcycle club it was, then. Was it wrong that she found the bikies better company than the wannabe boy band in the media lab?

Still, she wasn't stupid. A bunch of angry

men was still dangerous, even if she knew she wasn't responsible for whatever was wrong with their system. It had worked fine when she'd left, so they must have done something.

She sent out a prayer to the universe, to help her fix whatever they'd done without anything else going wrong.

THIRTEEN

The sun had barely set when Harlow heard Octavia's call. He was in the air at the speed of thought, heading inland.

He found her car parked outside a building surrounded by high walls, with bars on all the windows. Like a prison or a military fort. Lined up outside it were a number of two-wheeled conveyances that bore a passing resemblance to the swiftwalker he'd seen someone riding in

Glasgow, but if the swiftwalker was a deer after a long, hard winter, these things were fatted hogs, ready for slaughter. Did these perhaps possess an engine, like Octavia's car?

The garrison of this fortress – for the men outside looked like fighters – stood with their arms folded beside the conveyances, with the exception of one man who stood over Octavia, shouting at her.

How dare he try to intimidate a lady like that?

Harlow dropped to the road, folding his wings behind him, and marched into the fray. He strode past the garrison to stand at Octavia's shoulder, where he could meet the surprised gaze of the bully.

"Who are you?" the man demanded.

Octavia glanced back. Her eyes widened slightly at his appearance, but she recovered quickly. "This is Harlow. He's my assistant." She shrugged. "Now, do you want me to get to work on fixing your problem, or do you want to shout some more? I do charge by the hour, you know."

The man's face turned red. "This is your fault, so you'll be fixing it for free, or my boys will – "

Harlow stepped forward, so he stood toe to toe with the man. "I'd let the lady work, if I were you."

The man stepped back, then jerked his head at Octavia. "You, fix things. And you…do you know who I am?"

Harlow shrugged.

The man snapped his fingers. "Boys, show him."

Two men from the garrison stepped up. "Show some respect to the president of the Devil's Own Motorcycle Club!" one said, as his fellow sank his fist into Harlow's midsection.

Or he would have, if Harlow had been made of flesh and not living stone. Instead of knocking the breath from Harlow's lungs, it was his attacker who doubled over with a howl, clutching his smashed fist.

His companion was quick to respond – too quick, for he moved straight to anger, without realising how Harlow had hurt the other man. He went for Harlow's face, in a blow that likely would have broken a normal man's teeth. Instead, all that broke were his fingers.

"Deal with him!" the president shouted, waving more men forward.

In the past, Harlow had been in a few bar room brawls…usually instigated by Grant, and his part had mostly been hauling his brother out before he got himself killed. He'd learned to take blows where they would do the least damage, but now…he just stood unmoving, until the fools figured out they were wasting their time.

"OI!"

Octavia's shout cut through the noise. As one, they all turned to stare at her.

And the open door behind her.

The president's jaw dropped.

"I found your problem. Your batteries are flat. I plugged my phone in to get enough charge for the fingerprint scanner to work, but when the low battery light comes on, you need to replace the batteries, or this will happen again. So if you send someone down to the supermarket for some double As, I'll show you how to fit them so you won't need to call me next time." She looked askance at all the men on the ground, and Harlow standing in the middle of them, with his arms folded. "Or my assistant."

The president, who'd paled considerably, picked up his jaw and managed to find an uninjured man to send on Octavia's errand.

"While we're waiting, let's discuss my fee. I mean, there's my standard hourly rate, emergency call out rate, plus my assistant..." Octavia coughed. "Good tech support does not come cheap, Mr Jerome, as I'm sure you know."

After a long moment, Mr Jerome sent his men inside, though he stayed where he was until the errand boy returned, his swiftrider or whatever the conveyance was, growling like a bear beneath him. Harlow was fascinated by it. Perhaps he'd be able to obtain one. He'd have to ask Octavia how, though.

Octavia fitted the small cylinders into the lock she'd taken apart, explaining to both men what she was doing, before she reassembled the lock again and handed the remaining cylinders in their paper packaging to Mr Jerome. "Now, my fee?"

Mr Jerome sent the errand boy scurrying inside. He returned a moment later with a stack of brightly coloured notes that were evidently the money of this time, and handed them to Octavia.

Octavia tucked the money into her pocket and inclined her head. "A pleasure doing business with you again, Mr Jerome. You know how to contact me if you need any more technical support in future." She walked to her car with her head held high, then turned back. "Are you coming, Harlow?"

Flying was fun, but…it seemed prudent to accompany her right now, in case any of these men thought of coming after her in revenge. Then again, surely they'd want revenge on Harlow for humiliating them, though it was hardly Harlow's fault they'd punched him…

"Yes, ma'am," he said, sliding into the seat beside her. Did he imagine it, or did she drive a bit faster this time than she had the other night?

They'd been driving for at least a quarter of an hour before Octavia suddenly blew out a breath, then said, "Well, that was an adventure. Thank you for coming, by the way. Should I even ask how you knew I'd be there and need your help?"

Harlow shrugged. "You asked for help. I answered. I'm your gargoyle protector. It's what I'm bound to do."

She rubbed her hand across her forehead. "Yeah, you said that before, but I kind of…well, I honestly thought I was imagining you at first. Especially the way you disappeared that first night. But those men could see you, and hit you, and they didn't even hurt you.

You just appear out of nowhere, right when I need you and I have to wonder…why now? And where have you been all my life?"

Harlow wasn't entirely certain, but he could give her some answers. "You called me in the cemetery. Something you said woke me, and now when you call for help, I come."

She looked puzzled. "In the cemetery? You mean we actually managed to…wait, you said you arrived in the *Hooghly*, and Alethea said that cemetery's one of the oldest in Perth. Were you…did we wake up your corpse? Because you don't look dead."

Harlow had to think for a moment, before responding, "I believe I died in 1834, in the most foolish escapade my brother ever suggested. I feel more alive now than I ever did then, but I do not now how you managed to wake me. For death is not supposed to be just a sleep one can be woken from."

"Don't ask me. The only magic I'm capable of involves computers. Callie's the one who knows about witchcraft, though she's always said magic doesn't exist. Which is why it's even weirder that a spell she cast actually worked…and why me? We were trying to summon a demon to protect Alethea, not me. I didn't need protection. Well, until tonight, maybe. But…" She wet her lips. "Are you protecting all of us? Is that why you're here, and other times you're not?"

Harlow shook his head. "I am bound to protect you, and you alone. You woke me, and I answer your call for help, whatever help you might need. Whether it is in early colonial farming practices, or defending your person from some very angry, but not very bright men."

"Yeah, thank you for that. I'm not sure what would've happened if you hadn't shown up. Maybe I should just stick to remote tech support, and the occasional company contract. They don't pay as well, but…well, with the money I made today, I should have enough to replace my computer, and pay a courier to ship the graphics card here. Just crypto traders and fraudsters from here on in."

"If you wait until the evening to make house calls like these, I can go with you to protect you. You have only to say the word," Harlow said.

Octavia stared at him for a long moment, then turned her eyes back to the road. "I just…can't believe it. My own gargoyle protector. And you were on the *Hooghly*…" She gave a little laugh. "Is it wrong that I'm more excited about what you can tell me about the past? I mean, you were on the same ship as Sean Bell. Living in the same settlement as him. All the things I haven't been able to find in any written sources are there, in your head!"

"I will answer any questions you have. I am bound to serve, after all," Harlow said. But in his stone heart, he knew it was more than that. He wanted to be with her. Wanted to protect her. He wasn't madly in love with her like Stanley or Wystan had been with their women, but he greatly admired her. She was a lady scholar, her station so far above his own he didn't dare even think…

"First, though, you should probably come home with me. Or at least to the café, where we can talk without waking Rory or Tacey."

He could not refuse. Even if he'd wanted to.

FOURTEEN

"Hey, what do you know about *Hamilton*?" Octavia asked. She'd spent all night asking him about his time in Hooghly Town, as he called the encampment, that she'd forgotten he'd likely been alive at around the same time as the man the musical was about.

"Do you mean *General Hamilton*?" Harlow asked.

Octavia blinked. She'd seen the trailer, and

she vaguely remembered a glimpse of military uniforms. "I guess…"

Harlow grinned. "Ah, it was a fine ship, that one. American, out of New York. We spotted it just after we crossed the Equator. Captain Read came aboard with one of his passengers to trade and dine with our captain. He sold me a bottle of particularly fine gin, which I planned to drink when we finally received our land allocation, so I never did get to drink it. We parted ways and we all expected her to sail off, but instead we raced her, and were quite evenly matched for several days. Then we lost sight of her in the night, and near forgot about her what with Christmas and Hogmanay to celebrate."

Octavia couldn't help but laugh. "I didn't know there was a ship called that. The Hamilton I'm referring to is the man I imagine the ship was named after. They made a play, a musical about him, and it showed in New York. There's a recording that's meant to be streaming soon. We should watch it."

"You wish me to attend the theatre with you?"

She didn't know when theatres would be open again. That would depend on how long the pandemic persisted. Maybe until those boys were ready to actually perform their hideous rap parody of Peel's life.

"If they do make a musical about Thomas Peel's life, then I absolutely insist you come to the theatre with me, so you can tell me all the stuff they get wrong," Octavia said.

Harlow stared. "A theatre show about Thomas Peel? Why in heaven's name would anyone care? Even the man himself was a recluse who hated everybody."

Octavia began to explain about the boys in the computer lab, and their project.

Harlow only nodded, as if he understood. "Rich young fools, with more money than sense. But what I do not understand is why you do not seek the same assistance for your project. If you are raising money by doing business with questionable characters like Mr

Jerome and his band of bully boys, surely it would be safer to ask for your university to help? You are a scholar, just as they are, are you not?"

"Yeah, but..." Octavia hesitated. Callie loved being an academic, and both Catena and Alethea were planning on doing PhDs, but she couldn't see the point of continuing on the academic track past getting her bachelors degrees. The politics, for a start... She sighed. "If I ask for university funding for my project, as part of a PhD or another degree, then they own the commercial rights to it. My immersive world will be theirs to do with what they want, and after I graduate, I won't have any control over it, because it won't be mine any more. So even if those boys write a really good play that's really popular, they won't own it, not that it probably matters to them, because they don't need the money. The other problem is that they already have so much support, not just from the university but from government and industry, through their contacts. Their parents and the people they went to school with, mostly. So if a competing project that looks at the same time period, but in a different way, that's just being done by one person, which doesn't have any support from any other organisation, comes before them…why would they bother approving it? They've already supported the boys doing their group project, and they only have so much money to spend on research. I mean, they could be funding the cure for some disease, or an archaeological dig that's our only chance to learn something incredible, or…" Octavia sighed. "This is…just for me. I want to create this for me, more than I want it for anyone else. I want to show what the women in my family did. Their courage, the conditions they endured, the lives they lived…they did things I can only imagine, things I wouldn't dare."

It was Harlow's turn to laugh. "I doubt any of the women in Hooghly Town would have stood up to that band of men today the way you did, or talked to their leader like that, either. If anything, you are braver than any of the women in your family who came before you. Which is why you will complete this project, and I will do everything in my power to help you. All my memories are at your service. Those selfish young men don't deserve to succeed the way you do."

Octavia wasn't sure about any of that, but she figured it would be rude to say anything more than, "Thank you." Then they reached Bell House, and the sky was already lightening toward dawn. Definitely time for bed.

She leaned over and kissed his cheek. "Until tomorrow night, Harlow." Then she headed into the house.

FIFTEEN

The sun was setting as Octavia walked into the café. "What are you still doing here?" she asked Tacey.

Tacey looked up from the counter, revealing dark circles beneath her eyes. "Working. I guess I should close up now and take Rory home to bed."

"And get some sleep yourself, while you're at it," Octavia said, headed for the stairs.

"Oh, your computer parts arrived. I had the courier carry them upstairs for you," Tacey said.

Wow, that was quick. Maybe the stories about slow shipping weren't true. "Thanks." Octavia made her way upstairs.

Only to find Rory and her drawing supplies spread across the floor. "Auntie Octavia!" She threw herself around her knees, nearly tripping Octavia.

"Hey, so this is the way, huh? What are you drawing today?" Octavia asked as she untangled herself.

"Monsters. Good monsters," Rory said, pausing to sharpen her grey pencil. There was a lot of grey on the page.

Octavia picked up the nearest one. It looked a lot like Harlow. Well, it was grey and vaguely man shaped with either wings or a cape. "What's this one's name?"

"Mr Monster."

Of course.

"Your mum wants to go home for dinner

soon, so how about I help you pack all your stuff, so we can surprise her when she comes up and you're all ready to go?" Octavia suggested.

"Okay. Wystan usually does that, but he's hiding because you're here," Rory said.

Octavia reached for the pencil case. "Who's Wystan?"

"The monster who protects me from the bad monsters."

He sounded like Harlow, too, but it wasn't like Rory to make up names. She usually borrowed them from TV shows, and Octavia couldn't remember anyone by that name. Unless the character's name was actually Winston…

"Does your mum know about Wystan?" Octavia ventured.

"Yup. She lets him sit next to me in the car. Otherwise, he'd have to fly all the way home. He's not allowed in the house, though. He has to keep watch from the roof."

Like a gargoyle.

With Octavia's help, Rory was surprisingly efficient at packing up, so she was already sitting at the top of the stairs, waiting, when Tacey came to get her. She rose to her feet without anyone saying a word. "Come on, Mummy, let's go home. Wystan said he'd meet us in the car." She held out her hand to Tacey, who took it.

"You'll be all right here by yourself?" Tacey asked.

"Sure. I'll close up, and then spend most of the night putting my new toy together," Octavia said. True to her word, she followed them to the door and locked it behind them, before racing back up the stairs to watch them drive off. Was she imagining things, or was there a dark shadow in the back seat beside Rory? It was hard to see in the dark, but...

Tacey's car turned, and vanished from sight.

Octavia sighed, shook her head and got to work.

SIXTEEN

It was past midnight by the time Octavia had finished putting her new computer together, and then she still had to install all the software. Times like this, it would be nice to have someone to talk to.

"Harlow, are you there?" she asked softly.

A moment later, he stepped out of the wall, like it was a doorway and not solid stone. "Yes."

"How did you do that?"

"It is a gargoyle thing. We're made of stone, and can walk through stone, too."

"Weird."

"You wish for my help?" he asked eagerly.

"Actually, I was wondering what you do when you're not here with me," she admitted.

"During the day, I hide in the walls. Here, or in the cottage near your house. But after dark, I like to go up on the roof and look out over what the colony has become. There's so much more to see, and it's so different to what I remember. I feel like I could never look my fill, because there is just so much to see."

"Can you show me?" The words were out of her mouth before she'd really thought them through. No way was she climbing on the roof of the café. There were houses across the street that had gardens on the roof, so there must be a way up over there, but this place wasn't like that. She'd have to find a ladder or climb out the window and scale the downpipe or…

"Sure." Harlow wrapped his arms around her and pulled her over to the wall.

Octavia squeezed her eyes shut, trying to focus on the warm strength of Harlow's embrace and not the strangeness of passing through stone, until she felt the breeze on her face. Only then did she dare open her eyes. "Oh, wow."

She hadn't expected the roof to be flat. You could put a table and chairs or a sofa bed up here, and stay up all night, just watching the stars. Or Fremantle, because any way she looked, the view was nothing less than amazing.

"If Tacey knew the view up here was this good, she'd open up a rooftop deck, so people could sit up here. They'd never want to leave."

"This business is your sister's, is it not?" Harlow asked.

"The café is, yes. I pay part of the lease for the premises so I can use the studio upstairs. But now I'm wondering if I'm holding her business back, not letting her use the space for extra seating, or for a way to let her customers come and sit up on the roof…" The clink of glass had her looking straight down, into the courtyard below. A bunch of backpackers sat at an old picnic table, drinking beer. Then one of them used his beer bottle to squash a cockroach on the table.

Octavia shuddered. She hated cockroaches. If the backpackers was having another plague of them, Tacey would need to get Dave, their usual pest control guy, to come and inspect the café, to make sure none of the roaches had taken up residence here.

She blinked. For a moment, she fancied one of the backpackers looked like Tacey's ex, Matt. The one who'd gotten her pregnant with Rory, then tried to kill her. Only this guy was built like a bodybuilder, and Matt had always been kind of lanky. Not to mention the fact that he was in prison for attempted murder. So unless he had a twin brother who worked out, it had to be nothing but a coincidence.

Besides, when he picked up the beer bottle,

the cockroach scampered off, not dead at all. Matt would have killed it, like the psychopath he was, instead of letting it go.

"Octavia?"

Too late, she realised Harlow had been talking to her while she'd been daydreaming about a man who didn't deserve a moment of her time, let alone space in her head. Harlow on the other hand…he'd brought her up here and helped her more than she could say. He deserved all of her attention.

"Sorry. Just thinking about my sister and…stuff. What did you say?"

He inclined his head. "I asked about the name of the café. I know that much has changed between your time and mine, but in my time, it would have been terribly impolite to name a place the Shut Up Café. I was wondering why she would choose such a name."

Octavia laughed. "Oh, technically our mum chose the name, not us. Tacey's real name is Tacita. Mum thought she was going to be a boy, and she wanted to call him Tacitus, which in Latin means silent, but she swapped it to Tacita when she was born a girl. Only when you say it aloud, the way Mum said it when she was angry, it sounds more like tacete, which means to be silent, or shut up. It was a standing joke when we were growing up, because if Mum ever said her full name, Tacey went all quiet because she knew it meant she was in trouble for something. Tacey wanted to call the place Tacita's Café, so I pointed out that no one would ever pronounce it right, and Callie laughed and said we should just abandon the Latin and call it the Shut Up Café and be done with it. Sybil said it made her think the food or the drinks must be so good, everyone just shut up to enjoy them, or that the café was a nice, quiet place to bring your laptop to work. Plus, it was still called Tacita's Café, sort of, just a cool play on words that only a Latin scholar would truly understand."

Harlow just shook his head. "My brother Grant would have understood instantly. He learned Latin, though I never did."

"You have a brother? Where is he now?" Even as the words left her lips, Octavia regretted them. Harlow had lived two hundred years ago. His brother was probably long dead.

Harlow grimaced. Yep, she'd put her foot in her mouth, all right. Octavia opened her mouth to apologise for being so insensitive.

"Last time I saw him, he was on the roof of your house with my cousin, Wystan. Guarding the other women in your family."

Octavia's jaw dropped. His brother was still alive? And Wystan…where had she heard that name before? Then it clicked. "You mean Wystan, the monster my niece said is guarding her, is real?"

"Wystan is bound to protect the redhead, who I presume is your sister, Tacey. Perhaps he has extended his protection to her daughter, too. I do not know. I have not spoken to them since we arrived at your home. I've been busy helping you." But he wouldn't meet her eyes. Like he was hiding something…

"So Tacey has someone protecting her? That's such a relief. I mean, we all help her as much as we can, and she's totally kickarse all on her own, being a single mum and a business owner in between keeping all of us in line and Bell House in order, but sometimes I think it'd be nice if she had someone to take care of her, to take the load off her, like a real partner..." Then she caught sight of Harlow's face and trailed off.

She'd never seen his expression look so dark, not even when those bikies attacked him.

"Wystan lost his wife and daughter shortly before we left Scotland to come to the colony. His heart died with them, for he has mourned them every day since. What you suggest is simply not possible, for whatever heart he once had no longer beats, as he is now a gargoyle. Nor can I say how good a protector he will be, seeing as he did not manage to protect his family, who he loved with all his heart. He might be bound to protect your sister and her daughter, but he is not the man he once was. Even after he arrived in the colony, he would fall into terrible bouts of melancholy where he would speak to no one and it was clear his thoughts were miles away. His love for Effie, and then losing her, broke something in his mind. He could never love your sister, or be a husband to her."

Pity smote her hard. Poor Wystan, to lose his whole family. But if what Rory had said was true, then he was already protecting Tacey and Rory, no matter what Harlow said. But…marriage? To a gargoyle? Was that even possible?

"Do other gargoyles do that? Fall in love with humans, and marry them?" Her mind whirled. If they did, that meant they shared a bed. All those rock hard muscles…and what would their kids be like? Could gargoyles even have kids, or did they shoot blanks?

"I do not know of any who have," Harlow said stiffly.

"Yeah, but…how many gargoyles do you know? And how long have you been one?"

Octavia pressed.

"I have been a gargoyle for less than a week, as you well know, and I only know of three others – my brother, and my two cousins, who are bound to guard the other girls who were in the graveyard that night."

So the spell had been successful in summoning a protector for Alethea after all? Good, because Octavia still felt a bit bad about helping set up the dating profile that had lured in Alethea's stalker.

"So the only gargoyles you know have been gargoyles for less than a week, and the only women they've been around are my sister, my niece, and my two cousins?" Octavia pressed.

Harlow nodded.

"Well, none of them would marry a guy they'd only known for a few days. Callie might sleep with him, but she's more likely to curse him with something horrible. Which one's protecting Callie?"

Harlow grimaced. "My brother Grant is bound to the witch. I warn you, he will likely try to seduce her, as he charms all women, including the daughter of his tutor, Vicar Jordan. When the vicar found out, he tossed Grant out of his house, which was shortly after Wystan lost his wife, so we all moved into Wystan's cottage with him, and…" He coughed. "If your cousin spends too much time with my brother, her virtue will be in danger. Perhaps you should warn her."

Octavia could only laugh. "Oh, I think it's more likely you should warn him. If he pisses her off, she'll curse his stone dick off, followed by his wings and anything else he's particularly attached to."

The look of disapproval on his face only deepened. "If Grant has been foolish, then he undoubtedly deserves whatever the consequences might be. I will not save him again."

"So you saved him before?" From what she'd seen of Harlow so far, she'd believe it.

Harlow sighed. "I tried. Many times, I tried, but Grant would always emerge from one scrape, only to fall even more deeply into another, until the night that ill-omened raid got him killed. I tried to save him then, too, but I never saw the shooter until it was too late. Too late for him, and too late for me."

"Wait…someone shot you? And your brother? Were they ever charged for it?"

He lifted his shoulders in one big shrug. "I do not know. I've had little time to consider who killed us, let alone whether justice was done. More important is my responsibility to help and protect you." He shook his head. "The past is not important."

Octavia didn't agree. Then again, Harlow's killer was likely long dead, whether they'd been arrested or not. They'd probably turn over in their grave if they knew the men they'd killed were alive and well in the present day, protecting and possibly even seducing modern-day women.

Wait…was that what Harlow was trying to do to her? First winning her over with all the history she wanted, then defending her against all those bikies, and now taking her up to the roof to romance her under the stars?

At some point, he'd released her, so he no longer had his arms around her, but it still felt intimate, being alone with him up here where no one could see them. Well, except maybe the gargoyle statue on the roof across the street, that seemed to smirk at everyone.

"What about you and my…virtue?" Octavia asked. No fucking way was she telling him she was a virgin. She'd made that mistake with other guys in the past, and it had only made them more eager to get into her pants. Like there was some award for being first…

Harlow drew himself up. "I am your protector. As long as I am with you, you are in no danger."

Yeah, but that was what made the idea so intriguing. He was obviously built to protect, with all those muscles, so it stood to reason that he'd never hurt her. He might be the best lover a girl ever had – perfect for your first time, if you were a bit nervous and a lot worried and plainly terrified of pregnancy after what happened to Tacey…

But she barely knew him. And he had horns. He wasn't even human.

She bet he'd be amazing in bed, though…

Octavia shook her head. She couldn't believe she was even considering it, but now her mind had gotten hold of the idea, it wouldn't let go. Her eyes skimmed down to the low-slung waistband of his track pants, then dipped lower. There was a definite bulge there, visible even in those loose pants. So if he was proportionate everywhere, that meant down there he'd be…

Octavia swallowed. No way he'd fit. Shit, he'd probably hurt her, if he was that big. No. No, no, no, no, NOPE.

Harlow took a step toward her, his hand outstretched, palm up. "I promise you have nothing to fear from me. I will not hurt you, and I will not let anyone else hurt you, either."

Octavia recognised the truth when she heard it. And it was – as long as she kept away from his cock, she'd be fine. So she took his hand, and said, "Can we go back down now? I should check to see if my computer's done."

"As you wish."

Strong arms pressed her against his muscled chest, but it was the bulge nudging her belly that held her attention. Would it really be so bad? Callie and Tacey both said that bigger was better, and Harlow was huge. If there was a way for them to do it without hurting her, maybe…

She'd known the guy for a matter of days and already she was thinking of taking him to bed? She might not be seeing hallucinations, but she still might be going mad. Octavia gave herself a little shake, looking around the studio desperately for something to distract her.

"Oh, look, the software's installed. Now all I need to do is set it up…"

He released her and stepped back. This time, she noticed, and felt the loss, even if only for a moment.

History was what ignited her passion, and

bringing it to life. Not hot, hard men with enormous cocks. Or at least they hadn't before…

Octavia cursed under her breath. She'd gone and fallen for Harlow, hadn't she?

SEVENTEEN

"Gah, this is impossible!" Octavia exclaimed, running her hands through her hair in frustration. She must have been doing it a lot, seeing as there was little resistance and she vaguely remembered braiding it earlier. The braid and whatever she'd tied it with must have come loose hours ago.

"May I be of assistance?" Harlow asked.

Always with the good manners and polite

words. She wondered if he even knew any swear words – she'd never heard him say any.

"I need two things – Sean Bell, and the mill, and there's practically nothing about either of them! Not a single picture or record I can even use as a reference, except for a note on the original deed for the Bell estate that he arrived on the *Hooghly*, and that this was his land grant, given to him by the Governor in lieu of the one promised by Peel. But he's not on the passenger list, or the passenger lists for the *Gilmore* or the *Rockingham*, or any other ship that arrived before 1835. Yet his name is on a land grant and a marriage certificate when he married Carline Steel!"

Harlow froze. "He married Carline Steel?" He paused for a long moment. "I suppose if Stan died and didn't get her, some other man must have. I just never thought…" He shook his head. "Call me a coward, but I have no desire to be the man to tell Stan the woman he loved married another man."

Octavia had to admit she wouldn't want to,

either. Then she realised… "Stan is the cousin who's protecting Alethea, right? The girl who isn't living at Bell House with us?"

Harlow nodded. "He claimed her first."

What, like werewolves with their fated mates? That sounded…kinda creepy, but also kind of hot. Maybe she really was going mad.

"Well, if I know Alethea, and he asked her to find Carline, she would have done just that. I love history, and bringing it to people's attention, but Alethea's focus is on finding things, digging them up. That's why she studied archaeology. So if he's with Alethea, he probably already knows." Octavia wrapped her arms around herself. Oh, the heartbreak the guy must be feeling. She could scarcely bear it, and she'd never been in love. But it wasn't Carline, or Stan she wanted to know more about right now. She was supposed to be searching for… "Sean Bell. What do you know about him? He was on the ship with you, right?"

Harlow shook his head slowly. "I do not

recall anyone of that name aboard the *Hooghly*, or in Hooghly Town after. My first thought is that he was aboard the *Gilmore* and he died before we arrived, but you say he married one of your ancestors in 1835, so that does not seem possible. Unless he arrived on the *Rockingham* instead. That ship was wrecked in another bay further south, and they set up camp there, instead of with us." He spread his hands wide. "Forgive me, but I do not know this Sean Bell at all. I cannot help you."

"Maybe he went by another name, or came on another ship, but something happened, so he had to fudge the details, or there would have been trouble. I will…try again later. I guess we're at a dead end with him, for the moment." She pulled up the three pictures she had, and set them side by side. "Did you ever see the mill at Point Belches? We call it the Old Mill now, but I imagine it must have been new then. I have three pictures: Garling in 1827, Wittenoom in 1839 and Blundell in 1843. The only problem is that the current one, the one in the two later pictures, wasn't built until 1835 but apparently it was robbed in 1834. So either there was an earlier mill on the site, or this one was in use a year before it was officially opened, while they were still building it, or…I don't know." She wrung her hands. "I know you mostly lived down past Woodman Point, but is there any chance you remember the mill?"

A sad smile stole across his face, and her heart sank.

"You don't, do you?" she asked.

"Oh, I remember the mill very well. It's probably my last, clearest memory from that time. But I am a farmer, Octavia. Pictures are all good and well, but to truly show you what I remember, I need to have my feet on the ground. If you take me there, I will tell you everything I know, and then you will know how the mill was robbed in 1834."

Octavia grabbed her keys, then thought for a moment and seized her camera bag and phone, too. "Let's go."

They drove in silence for most of the way, until the river came into view.

Harlow's breath hissed out. "This is the Swan River of your time?"

It would have all been dark then, in his time. Two million people, electricity, and two centuries later...she couldn't imagine how unrecognisable it would be to his eyes.

"That's Melville Water. All along the edges, all the way from Darling Scarp to the sea, south to Mandurah and north to...actually, I'm not sure how far north the city goes now, but definitely up to Alkimos...it's all the suburbs of the city of Perth. Two million people live here, with another million scattered around the state." She reached for his hand and squeezed it. "All this made possible by the people who arrived here a couple hundred years ago and saw the Swan River for its possibilities. People like you, and my ancestors."

Harlow just shook his head. "None of us ever envisioned anything like this. This city would rival London..."

Octavia hid a smile. "London in your time, definitely. Less than two million people lived there then. Now, I think it's seven or eight million."

More headshaking. "The biggest city I ever saw was Glasgow."

"I think that's about the same size as Perth. Maybe a little smaller. I'd have to look that up."

"And the bridges over the river," he breathed. "With trains!"

The Perth to Mandurah line did look pretty, all lit up like that, as the train raced along the freeway.

He still hadn't let go of her hand. Luckily, her car wasn't a manual, so she could drive one-handed just fine.

"And there's the Old Mill," she said softly, as the well-lit white tower came into view, dwarfed by the enormous pine tree beside it. "There are coloured lights on the tree, but they only turn them on around Christmas. Then it becomes the biggest Christmas tree in the whole city."

She took the exit, and coasted beneath the Narrows Bridge.

"The city…the towers!"

Even her breath caught in her throat as she saw the illuminated CBD reflected in the river at night. "On a still night, you can get the most amazing photos here. All along the South Perth shoreline, actually. Sometimes even with dolphins." She'd seen the dolphins once or twice, but never managed to actually photograph them. Wildlife photography wasn't really her thing. People and places, sure, but anything that moved fast and didn't do what it was told…yeah, she had no chance of getting a picture of it.

"You would have seen them that night in the cemetery, up close," she said slowly.

Harlow nodded. "Yes, but it's different from the air. They're down below and you're trying to come to terms with your wings and being alive and the pull to protect…I did not have time to stare at the city then, as I do now."

Seeing things from the air before the ground…and knowing so much about the past, then waking in this far-flung future as a completely different creature…it was weird enough just thinking about it. Octavia couldn't imagine how much harder it must be for Harlow.

"We can park the car here, if you want, just so you can take it in. Or we could walk up to the top of the bridge, to give you a better view." It wasn't like she needed him to remember everything about the mill right this moment. They had all night.

"Here…is good."

So she parked the car under the bridge, nodding to the fishermen camped out along the edge, and led Harlow up the steps to the pedestrian path on the side of the Narrows Bridge. He stared around, still not saying anything, trying to orient himself.

Octavia pulled out her phone, and found a compass app. "That way's north." She pointed.

"That's the way we came, with Melville Water over there, and if you keep following the river, that's the way back to Fremantle. That's Mount Eliza, which we call Kings Park. Perth City, of course, and Perth Water all the way up to Heirisson Island, where there's now a causeway bridge across the river, too. This one's the Narrows Bridge, between Perth City and South Perth, which is all along the shore here." She wasn't sure what else to point out.

"And that's the mill, which you call the Old Mill, though it is new to me. The mill that stood on that spot in my time was made of wood, not whitewashed stone." Harlow pointed slowly at each of the outbuildings. "None of these were here. The only permanent structure was the mill itself. The miller and his sister slept in a tent, over there." He pointed across the bridge, to the boat ramp. "That's where the boats loaded and unloaded wheat and flour, but William Steel tied his own boat up in the mill pond, which was open to the river then." He swallowed.

"That's where we brought our boat in, too, but we dragged it ashore and hid it in the bushes. It was supposed to be easy, a quick raid. In and out and gone, with no one the wiser. Stan's idea, but Grant and Wystan agreed to it. I only went along to keep them from getting into trouble, and you can see how well I managed that." He let out a bitter laugh. "Some protector I was."

Octavia's blood ran cold. "What are you saying?"

He pointed at a patch of bushes. "There were bushes there, then, too. That's where we hid while we waited for William Steel to leave. Three of us to raid the mill, while Stan went to get Carline. Only there was an armed man in the mill, and we didn't see him until it was too late, and he'd already shot Grant. I ran out to drag him to safety, and he shot me, too. I didn't see what happened to Stan or Wystan, but as they rose as gargoyles with me, I can only guess that they died, too. Someone buried us in that cemetery, where you woke us."

Horror stole her voice. "You mean this is where you died?" Her words came out as a whisper.

Harlow bowed his head. "Where all four of us died because of a stupid scheme we'd thought up in a tavern. We should have been headed home to start building on our land grants, which we'd finally received that very day, but we were fools. All of us. And now…we have nothing. Not our lives or our land, and the world has changed so much, there is no place for four early colonial farmers, except to satisfy the curiosity of historians, like yourself."

"Oh, Harlow…" She couldn't help it. She hugged him.

Only to have him push her away. "I don't deserve your pity. Did you not hear me? We were thieves, or would-be thieves, who were shot to protect the miller's property. If we hadn't been killed, we would have been sent to Van Diemen's Land as prisoners."

"But there's no record of any of it. There

was one raid on the mill, and the Governor used it as justification for the Pinjarra Massacre, where Peel and his buddies went down to the Murray River and slaughtered Aboriginal men, women and children. I've seen it on the signs inside the mill…" Signs that were all inside the fenced-off complex that protected the mill from night time visitors. Octavia sighed.

"Show me."

"The signs are inside the security fence. It's only open a few hours a week, on particular days. I'll go back during the week, when it's open, and take photos of all the signs for you."

"Or we could go now."

His arms encircled her, before his wings spread on either side of them and they soared into the air…over the fences, to stand before the closed doors of the mill itself.

"We can't be in here!" Octavia hissed. If anyone caught them, they'd get arrested.

"Show me these signs, and then I shall fly us out of here," Harlow said.

She marched past two signs, before she found the one she wanted. "There." While Harlow read it, she snapped a picture with her phone, then went back and photographed the others, too. "This one mentions the first mill was destroyed in a fire."

"That wasn't me. The last thing I saw before I closed my eyes for the last time was the mill, still standing."

But it was important, she was sure of it. She didn't know why or how or even where it fit into the overall scheme of things, but something about the fire pinged at her intuition, or whatever you called it when an idea wouldn't let go.

"Hey, you're not allowed to be in there!"

Fuck. Security.

Two rent-a-cops in a hatchback smaller than Octavia's, carrying bright torches that probably doubled as batons, when they weren't shining the light right into her eyes, blinding her.

Harlow's arms wrapped around her again, and he leaped into the air.

EIGHTEEN

Harlow knew he didn't deserve the pleasure he felt at holding Octavia in his arms, but right now, he didn't care. He was going to hold her and fly with her and protect her, all at once.

The men's torches followed him into the air, so he darted behind the mill, where they couldn't see him, then banked right to slip between the branches of the dark pine tree. He landed where a particularly thick branch met the trunk, wide enough for Octavia to stand with both feet, as he spread his wings wide to hide her from sight. No shooter would hit Octavia tonight – and the bullets would not hurt him now, either.

An eternity passed, or so it seemed, while the men argued about what they'd seen and whether they should enter the compound to search for trespassers. Neither of them had the keys to the gate, as it turned out, and neither pulled out a weapon, either, so once they were finished arguing, they climbed back into their tiny car and drove off, albeit very slowly.

"I think they're gone. I can't even see the glow of their headlights around the corner any more," Octavia said.

"You wish for me to fly you down?" Harlow asked.

"Yes, that would be nice. I'm not much good at climbing trees, and this one's really high." She swallowed.

"A few more minutes, to see if they return. If I were responsible for patrolling a place like this, I would double back, to catch the criminals just when they thought they were safe."

Actually, he never would have thought of such a thing, if he hadn't seen it on one of the TV shows Octavia and her niece watched.

Plus it allowed him to hold her in his arms for a little longer…

Finally, he could delay no longer, and he glided them down to the footpath beside Octavia's car. While they flew, her arms had found their way around his neck and he would have given anything to keep them there. Her body was so soft and warm and lovely…

Oh, but her lips on his cheek were softer still, so lovely his breath caught in his throat. "I think you're a perfectly good protector. You couldn't possibly have thought of everything, and you said it wasn't even your idea. You can't protect fools from their own stupidity. That's Murphy's Law, isn't it? That if there's more than one way to do something, someone, somewhere will find a way to do it so utterly wrong, it'll result in catastrophe."

"I have never heard of such a law."

Octavia laughed softly. "Maybe it was after your time. Anyway, you said you waited until the miller was gone and only Carline was home. You couldn't possibly have known…oh!"

"What is it? Are you hurt?"

She shook her head. "This is Carline Bell we're talking about, isn't it? Crack shot with a rifle, who'd greet uninvited guests on her steps with a gun beside her. She was a legend in the colony. What if she was the shooter, and there wasn't anyone else? Because a woman alone out here, even I'd be inclined to shoot first and ask questions later. Maybe she shot you, and then took your bodies out to the cemetery to bury the evidence, which is why no one knew about your raid."

Harlow could only shake his head. "Carline was just a slip of a girl. There is no way she could have carried one of us anywhere, let alone all four. She might have been the one who shot me, but she had to have help rowing the bodies up the river to the cemetery, and burying them."

"Her brother, maybe? You said she had a brother. And there was Sean Bell, remember. She married him about then. Maybe he helped her, too."

Harlow wasn't sure if he felt better or worse, knowing he'd likely been killed by the woman they'd come to carry away. They'd had no intention of harming her…all Grant had wanted was the flour in the mill. Stan would have treated her like any stolen bride back in Scotland. It was such a time-honoured tradition, it had never occurred to any of them that she might object to being stolen.

"Fools. We were such fools," Harlow said.

And he was the biggest fool of all…not for what he'd done then, but for the thoughts he couldn't seem to banish now. Thoughts of Octavia in his arms, with no clothes between them. Stealing her for a bride of his very own…

If only she'd agree and not emulate her ancestress in trying to shoot him.

134

NINETEEN

The sky was already lightening by the time Octavia pulled up outside Bell Cottage, but she didn't want to part from Harlow. She ached to feel his arms around her again, and she didn't think he should be alone right now. Not with all the things he'd revealed tonight…

But while she was still wrestling with whether she should invite him inside, Harlow had already made the decision for her.

He bowed. "Until tomorrow night, Octavia. Should you have need of me, I shall take shelter in the ruined cottage."

Carline's cottage. The last place he should be, after learning that she'd likely been the one who shot him.

But he'd already departed, and dawn was approaching. She was too late. If only she'd had the courage to say what she wanted on the way home…

But she couldn't even say the words in her head, let alone out loud. Because they were crazy of course.

What kind of mad person wanted to take a monster to bed, let alone hand him her v-card?

This was all his fault, being so heroic and all. When he'd flown her up into that tree, holding tight to her with his hard body pressed against hers, all she'd been able to think about was climbing him like a tree. By the time he'd brought her down to the ground again, her underwear was soaked through and she didn't want to let go of him. If there hadn't been a bunch of fishermen under the bridge, she might have surrendered to the desire to make out with him in the car.

And now, here she was, at home alone, about to go to bed alone, but there was no ignoring her soaking wet knickers or the deep ache inside. Even if she couldn't say the words, her body knew what it wanted: Harlow, in every possible way.

Maybe it was time to get that vibrator out of the box, and actually use it.

She'd bought it after talking to a couple of girls at another mine site. They'd been mourning their inability to maintain a normal relationship with anyone, what with their fly-in-fly-out schedules making them spend so much time at the mine site, and then one of the cleaners had told them they didn't need a man to make them happy – they should do what the American girls did, and buy a vibrator. Guaranteed orgasms, and you never had to wash anyone else's socks, or listen to him mansplain anything. So Octavia had bought one on the way home, but the infernal device was still in the box, in the bottom drawer beside her bed.

She'd taken it out once, but it had looked so big and intimidating. It hadn't helped that she'd bought a metallic silver one, instead of emerald green or the even more daunting flesh-coloured ones.

Now, in the dim predawn light, it looked more grey than silver. Like the stone skin of a gargoyle. And bigger than she remembered.

She flicked it onto the lowest setting, letting it hum in her hands for a moment before she brought it to the apex of her thighs. The humming head teased her clit, so she pressed it against herself a little harder, until she had to bite her lip to keep from crying out as the first orgasm hit.

Now she understood what the other girls had meant about guaranteed orgasms. She didn't even have to push it inside her to feel…to feel…

The second one took longer than the first,

but it was quickly followed by a third. If she hadn't been soaking wet before, she definitely was now. But now she was aching even more to feel Harlow inside her, when all she had was this dick shaped device and a bottle of lube she wasn't sure she even needed right now.

She debated whether to put the vibrator away and go to sleep, or to try and satisfy the itch Harlow had left her with.

She'd broken it out of the box. May as well try out all the functions before she put it back…

But she wasn't that brave. She held the head against her clit, feeling another orgasm building. Would sex with Harlow be this good? Or would her first time hurt, like it did for most girls? Maybe he'd be willing to go slow. To just rub her clit until she was really panting for him and then…

She felt the fourth orgasm building, and she knew if it was Harlow's hands on her, she wouldn't want him to stop. She'd want him to take her, to take everything, as he gave her rush after rush of pleasure. If his hands were on her now, giving her this orgasm, she'd be begging. Begging him to thrust deep…

Before she could lose control completely, she pushed the vibrator inside. Slowly, because she wasn't even sure if the thing would fit, and she hadn't used any lube and it might hurt and…

OH. MY. GOD.

When she'd pushed it in all the way, a little vibrating nub at the base collided with her clit. Between that and the whole, humming length stretching her from the inside, she couldn't resist being catapulted into the stratosphere. She had to clap a hand over her mouth to muffle her scream.

For a moment, she lay there, helpless, still seeing stars, until she felt yet another orgasm building. Her body felt limp, wrung out, and yet she wanted this more than anything she'd ever wanted before. She wanted all the orgasms Harlow could give her. With his hands and his hard cock and maybe even his mouth…

The next, shuddering orgasm brought tears to her eyes. More than anything, she wanted to feel this with Harlow, not some battery-operated piece of plastic.

With shaking hands, she switched it off, and let it slide out of her onto the bed. That had been…amazing and disappointing in equal measure.

She wiped down the vibrator and put the box away in the back of the drawer, vowing never to use it again. Because despite all those orgasms, she still ached, and she knew in her heart no one could soothe that ache but Harlow. The monster protector she wanted more than anyone else, if only he'd have her.

TWENTY

By the next evening, Octavia had managed to get her raging hormones under control. Or she thought she had, until she was in the studio with Harlow, as she tried and failed to concentrate on creating the pilot for her little virtual world. As with the original pilot, she'd tried to focus on just Fremantle, but the more she thought about it, the more she wanted the mill and Clarence or Hooghly Town or whatever the place was called in there, too.

Harlow's hand appeared over her shoulder. "You should make those tents more brown. The canvas was cream to start with, but under a tree, wherever the leaves fell or when it rained, they started to turn brown. Much like the Swan River, when you look at it up close."

Octavia nodded, trying not to think of what else she wanted Harlow to do with that hand. With both his hands, and every other part of him.

It hadn't helped that she'd dreamed about him, too, and the dreams had been far more lurid than anything she'd imagined.

So with him so close now, it was driving her mad with want. Or lust. Or some other inexplicable urge to jump his bones. She'd never understood the phrase before, but now she wanted it, it made perfect sense.

Finally, she shook herself. "Can we go out to Hooghly Town again? I'd like to get some photos I can use for the topography, as a base for the background before I try to recreate the town, and if you can tell me what was where as I do it, I can record your commentary so I can work on this during the day when you're not around, too."

"If that is what you wish, then that is what we shall do."

Was he reading her mind or something? Because her wishes were definitely way past a PG rating and rapidly sinking into R territory. She prayed he couldn't read her mind.

"Right. Just let me get my camera gear and a tripod, and we can go." If she was lucky, the fresh ocean breeze would blow some sense into her head. Or at least blow some of these lustful thoughts out of it.

The full moon was still high in the sky when they pulled into the car park, silvering the landscape like early morning frost. With the sky so clear on a winter's night, there might well be frost by morning.

"Please promise you won't vanish on me this time," Octavia said.

"I cannot apologise enough for that. I will

never let dawn creep up on me again. Here, let me carry those for you." He held out his arms.

She relinquished the tripod and, after a moment's hesitation, the heavier of her two bags. Then she paused to slip into the harness that held her action camera, and switched it on. Now she'd at least have a record of whatever Harlow told her about what had once happened here, so if her pictures tonight didn't turn out, she could come back in daylight for a reshoot.

The cemetery was their first stop. She'd read about it in the archaeology reports, but it was different standing there in that miserable bowl where the ocean breeze could not reach, as Harlow told her about the men, women and children he'd buried beneath the golden sand.

Now she understood why he hadn't been able to move from this spot the first time. It wasn't long before she couldn't even see the camera for the tears streaming down her face. All because of Thomas Peel and his desire for wealth, he'd brought them here to their deaths, not caring for their plight in the place that was nothing like he'd promised.

Through his conceit and negligence, Peel had murdered these people. Octavia only wished he was still alive so he could be brought to justice, but it would be two hundred years too late for these people.

"What sort of grave markers did you give them?" she asked. It was one thing that hadn't been in any of the reports, and she'd always wondered.

"Wooden crosses, mostly, or ones made of seashells, laid over the grave. There wasn't much stone to be had, and no money to send to Fremantle for a stonemason to carve a proper gravestone. Heaven knew Peel owed it to them, but the only thing he cared about was the land he felt the Governor owed him, which he believed he'd been cheated out of, and that's what he told us. It wasn't until some of the Governor's men came to the camp in answer to the many letters people had sent, to see the squalor for themselves, that we learned the truth. Peel's ships had arrived late, weeks after the date they were supposed to arrive, so he was lucky to receive any land at all, let alone the acres he'd forfeited by the delay." Harlow just shook his head.

"I wonder what the early colony would have been like if the settlement scheme had been run by a better man than Peel. Someone who could have made it succeed. We might never have had convicts, or many of the other mistakes that were made in the first fifty years of the colony," Octavia said.

Harlow shrugged. "That's something for scholars like yourself to think about, not a simple farmer like me. I can only tell you what did happen, as I remember it."

Octavia shook her head. "I'm sorry. I don't mean to sound ungrateful. The information you have given me is far more than I could have ever hoped for. Details no one else knows…things no one else could have known, without standing here, in that time. You are a treasure, Harlow. Far more than just a simple farmer, because you're now the foremost expert on all things rural from two centuries ago."

Harlow snorted. "Don't be so free with the compliments yet. You haven't seen the house we lived in. Well, it was little more than a tent, really…"

He led her out of the graveyard and further along the trail, urged on by the breeze at their backs.

TWENTY-ONE

Harlow pointed out what looked like a pile of shells and limestone concreted together with sand, explaining that the concrete was in fact lime made from burned shells, which he and his brother had used to create a solid floor on which they'd erected a large canvas tent. They'd clubbed together with the other men from the *Hooghly* to build a row of cottages, all with limestone shell floors, and hearths built separately along the road, for they'd already experienced two bushfires carelessly lit by their fellow settlers, and had no desire to see another.

He paused, expecting Octavia to have a thousand questions, all of which he was only too happy to answer for her, if it was within his power, but she was frowning down at the small tablet she called her phone. "Those idiots," she muttered.

"Who? What's happened?" he asked.

Octavia blinked. "Sorry, I just got an update on my phone from one of the student group chats. The idiots who are making a musical theatre piece to celebrate Peel's life received word today that the Bicentennial Council has approved their grant. Everyone's congratulating them and saying they can't wait to see the show. Which means they'll all go and watch it, believing Peel to be some unsung hero, and if they even see my project, they won't believe it. Instead, they'll accuse me of lying, and try to destroy me on social media."

All her hard work, telling the truth about history, only to be accused of lying about it? No, Harlow would not allow it. He would protect her from this, too. "Well, then there's only one thing you can do, isn't there?"

"There is?"

"You need to show everyone your virtual world before their play is ready, so when they do go to the play, they already know the real story."

"But…the grant…and the support of the Bicentennial Council…"

"The Bicentennial is nine years away, if you mean two hundred years from 1829. Surely you will have this ready long before then. Are there not other ways you can show it to the world? So much is available on your internets. I have seen the miracles you work with only your phone, the information you can find almost instantly. Could you find a way to show people your virtual world on the internets?"

Octavia looked thoughtful. "That's what I'd originally intended, before I heard about the

Bicentennial, and the grants they were offering. But yeah, there are other ways. I could gamify the content somehow, and release it on Steam or some other online platform, like that immersive flyover of Ancient Rome. There are crowdsourcing sites, too, but I'd have to ask Rochelle for marketing advice on how to make those work, plus I'd still have to have a pilot for people to sample before they gave me their money."

"Will your friend help you?" He would, of course, but all he could help her with was the history. Using modern technology like one of the people of her time was not something he was good at.

"Well, Rochelle does owe me a favour, for letting her stay in the studio when I was up north and she was having trouble with her ex. She's brilliant with a camera, too, and she knows her way around some of the software, so if she had time and she was willing, maybe she'd be able to help. But there's only so much camera work that can be done for this project.

Like you said last night, so much of Perth had changed that it was hard to see anything of what it had been in those early days. What I'd really need is an artist who could draw what you remember, well enough for it to be digitised. I guess I could ask Ben, Rochelle's new boyfriend, if he's interested. He works at the café as Tacey's artist in residence in the evenings, so I could ask him the next time he's in…" Octavia's eyes fixed on Harlow's face, and she beamed. Then she threw her arms around his neck. "Thank you! I think this might actually work, thanks to you!"

He opened his mouth to tell her she was very welcome, or that it was nothing, because he'd do anything for her, but no sound came out. Instead, he kissed her.

TWENTY-TWO

The moment his lips touched hers, time stopped. There was no one and nothing else – just the two of them in the moonlight, with a world of longing she would finally see satisfied. She'd half expected him to feel like stone or a statue, but he was all man – hot and hard and strong, everywhere she needed him to be. And his hands…he held her like she was made of precious porcelain…but also like he never wanted to let her go.

She didn't want him to. Not now, not ever.

This was better than she'd ever dreamed he could be. Which made her wonder whether he'd be even better in bed…

Harlow broke the kiss, long before she was ready for him to stop.

"You're shivering. I'm living stone, so I barely feel the cold, but it must be close to freezing out here tonight. We should go back to your studio, or your home, where you can warm up, out of this winter weather."

Octavia touched a hand to her cheek. Her fingers were icy, and her cheek wasn't that much warmer. She'd been so focussed on how heated things were getting between them, she'd barely noticed the cold until now.

But now she did…she couldn't stop shivering.

"Here, I'll take you to the car." He scooped her up, camera bags and all, and took to the air. A moment later, he touched down beside the car. "Will you be able to drive? I could fly you if you can't."

She swallowed. "There's heating in the car. If we get in, and I turn the engine on, it'll warm up quickly, and I'll be fine."

Her head still whirling with euphoria from his kiss, Octavia barely noticed where they were going until she pulled up outside the café instead of her house. Maybe this was best. There was no one here, and they had the rest of the night…

"We need to get you inside, out of the cold," Harlow said, lifting her in his arms again.

He carried her upstairs, then set her down, but he didn't let go.

"Are you all right?" he asked, worry darkening his eyes.

She shook her head. "I want you to keep kissing me."

"Are you sure?"

"Fuck, yes, Harlow. I want you to kiss me and not stop." This time, she wrapped her arms around his neck and kissed him.

Just as perfect as the first time…

In a blissful daze, she stripped off her coat and toed off her shoes. Her shirt followed them to the floor.

"Octavia, your…you…you're perfect." He cupped her breasts in reverent worship, as she struggled to get rid of the bra next.

Pants, pants…his or hers? Hers, definitely. Jeans took a little more work than track pants, after all. But she managed to step out of them, still kissing him.

"This is madness, but I want to take you to bed. I shouldn't…as your protector, I mustn't…" he began between kisses.

"I want this, too. Just as much as you do. Take me to bed, Harlow. Please." God, was she begging? She was, and it felt right. Everything felt right. His hands beneath her arse as he lifted her, carried her to the bed, and set her down so carefully. The dark desire in his eyes as he crawled up the bed to kneel between her parted thighs, before he dipped his head to turn that wicked mouth on her breasts.

She arched her back, moaning as he sucked on one nipple, then the other, stroking her with both hands. Was it possible to come from him just playing with her breasts? She didn't think it was, but God it felt good. So good she wanted his hands to dip lower, into…shit, she still had her underwear on. That had to go.

She wriggled out of her knickers and tossed them onto the floor. "Please, Harlow," she begged.

He reached for her cheek and kissed her again, slow and languorously.

She liked his kisses well enough, but she wanted more. More than just kisses and caresses. She wanted…

A thick finger slid between her thighs, stroking her from the inside. "I've never known a woman to be so wet before," he marvelled.

"Because I want you!"

A second finger joined the first, before his

thumb pressed against her clit. Octavia didn't have words any more – the only sound that left her lips was an incoherent moan as he pleasured her, far more thoroughly than any machine could. She came so hard she saw stars for a moment, before Harlow's grinning face came into view.

"I think you must be the most beautiful woman I've ever seen right now. I could pleasure you all night, and all tomorrow, too. But what I really want is to make love to you, to take you as a man takes his wife. But as we are not wed, I would not wish to ruin you, or leave you with child. I would never forgive myself if…"

"Condoms. In the drawers, over there," Octavia breathed, pointing. "It's a sort of sheath you fit over your cock so the girl doesn't get pregnant. People have been buying them for me since Tacey got pregnant with Rory. Use whichever one you like. I swear, I probably have a lifetime's supply of the things in here."

Harlow opened first one drawer, then the one beneath it. "There's nothing in here," he said.

She sat up. That wasn't possible.

Except…it was. There wasn't a single condom in any of the drawers, or the cupboard, either. Surely Rochelle and Ben hadn't…she'd only been away a few weeks. No one could possibly have used that many condoms. No one.

Unless the burglar who'd broken her computer had stolen them?

What kind of nutjob stole novelty condoms, for fuck's sake?

"I'll buy some in the morning, so tomorrow. Tomorrow we can…"

He cut her off with a kiss. "Then I shall pleasure you all night. I can wait."

Even as they returned to bed, his fingers worked their magic, so the complaint on the tip of her tongue that she didn't want to wait was lost in a moan of pure pleasure, and she surrendered to him completely soon after.

Her only other coherent thought that night was that Harlow was so much better in reality than her dreams could ever have imagined.

TWENTY-THREE

Up close, Ben was younger than she'd realised. Oh, she'd seen him at the back of the café, sketching customers and adding more artwork to the walls, but she'd been more focussed on her customers than whatever he was doing. She knew Tacey had some sort of business arrangement with him that meant he had a permanently reserved table in the corner by the window, and that his presence tended to help when male customers tried to cause trouble, but now she looked at him, she had to wonder how anyone was frightened off by this cheerful boy.

Now, if he was built like Harlow, it would be a different story, but Ben looked like he could have been one of the high school kids from the art college up the road.

"Now, you never come over here to look at my art, and I know I haven't ordered anything this evening, so to what do I owe the pleasure of your attention?" Ben asked.

He sounded a little like Harlow, but there was no threat in his tone. Just an easy, open smile.

No way someone this young would be a history buff, or even want to be involved in her project. He probably didn't even know when the Swan River Colony had been founded.

But she had to ask.

"I was wondering whether you take commissions?" she asked.

"Of course, but you're Tacey's sister, and café staff. I'd be happy to sketch you while I'm here, like I have the other girls. Tacey usually puts them all on the wall behind the counter, but if you'd like to take your sketch home, I don't mind." He picked up a pencil and sketchpad and began to draw.

"No, no, it's not me I wanted. I'm trying to recreate a particular period in history, and I have a few watercolours and paintings from that time, but not much else to work with. What I do have is some oral history accounts, and I'm hoping to find someone who can help me turn the descriptions into pictures I can use to create a virtual world, to show people what the early Swan River Colony looked like." She kept her eyes fixed on the table, so she wouldn't have to see the rejection on his face. Hearing it would be enough.

"That sounds fascinating."

It took her a moment for his words to actually sink into her brain, and another moment before she could force her gaze up to meet his eyes. He really did look intrigued. "You'll help me?" she stammered.

"Perhaps. First, I'd like to see what sort of art style you're looking for, not to mention which medium. I prefer pencil and paper, but Rochelle talked me into buying a tablet, so I'm now experimenting with a little digital art, but I'm by no means an expert at it. Rochelle knows all kinds of art software, which is why I would have thought you'd ask her, not me." He raised his eyebrows, as if waiting for an explanation.

"I want to ask Rochelle to help, too, but more with the marketing and video side of things. It's the actual world that…well, it's probably easier if I just show you. Can you come upstairs for a minute?"

Ben nodded and followed her. He glanced around the studio for a moment, before turning his attention back to her. "This is your studio, where Rochelle stayed for a while."

"Yes."

"Then I believe I owe you an apology, or

perhaps payment of some kind. You see, Rochelle and I may have used one of your condoms one night. We bought our own the very next day, and the rest of your collection was safe, but Rochelle wasn't able to find a replacement for the one we used. I would like to offer you money to pay for it, if you'd only tell me how much."

Octavia's breath caught in her throat. "One condom. You used one condom?"

"Yes. I would not normally use someone's property without permission, but you weren't here and things were quite heated and it became rather urgent…" Ben coughed. "I didn't imagine you'd want it back after what we did with it."

No, she definitely didn't want anyone's used condoms. That was just…ew. But if he'd only used one…that meant it had to be the burglar. Who the fuck broke into cafés and stole condoms?

"It's…fine. Really. I hope you had fun," Octavia managed to say.

"Of course." Ben grinned, suddenly a man and not a boy any more. There was something almost predatory in that smile. Or maybe it was just knowing. "But I don't believe you wish to discuss my sexual exploits. You mentioned an early colonial history project?"

With relief, Octavia turned to her computer. "Well, this is what I have for Fremantle…" She pulled up the render for it, and panned around. "I'm starting to piece together the Old Mill in South Perth, and just this week, I've been working on Clarence, where the colonists from the *Hooghly* and the *Gilmore* first came ashore." She showed him the photographs she'd stitched together, with the tents she'd started to sketch in, based on George Bayly's picture of what he called Hooghly Town.

He stared at it hungrily. "One of my family arrived here on the *Hooghly*. I wonder if you've come across him in your research. Name's Steel."

Her breath caught in her throat. "Steel?" she managed to say.

"Yes. Stanley Steel, though he went by Stan."

Her breath hissed out. Not Harlow, then. But he had mentioned he had a cousin called Stan…

"I think I might remember that name from one of the passenger lists," she said slowly. She definitely didn't want to tell him his ancestor might be flying around on gargoyle wings right now. No way would he believe her.

"Yeah, I saw those, too. Problem is, he disappeared soon after he arrived and no one ever heard from him again. No death record, nothing. It's like he just vanished."

Her heart sank. So Carline probably had covered up the killing of Harlow and his family. If there were no records that Ben could find, searching for his ancestry, then there likely wouldn't be any for Harlow or the others. If she ever met Stanley Steel, she'd tell him he had a descendant living in the city, who was looking for him. Then Ben wouldn't believe she was mad, and Stan could make contact if he wanted to. Much better than blurting out that not only did monsters exist, but they came into the café on a regular basis.

"Well, record keeping wasn't the best back then. Lots of bushfires, living in tents…it's a wonder we have as much information as we do," Octavia said.

"Yes. The early colony here was a rough place," Ben said, still staring at the screen. He sounded like he actually knew something about Perth's history. Well, it was worth a shot.

"I wonder…in your research, have you come across a man named Sean Bell?" she asked.

Ben blinked. "Matter of fact, I think I have. Not so much the historical stuff, but in a book Callie gave me. I have a copy on my tablet, if you'd like to see it. I left it downstairs in my satchel."

Back down the stairs they went, for Ben to find Callie's book. If Callie had been home instead of away at a wedding, it might have been easier to ask her, but if Ben had actually found Sean Bell, when she never had…

"Ah, here it is. Sean Bell, written in on the page with the demon summoning spell."

Octavia choked. "What sort of spell?"

"One for summoning demons, apparently. Hang on, I think Callie sent me the translation, too. I didn't really pay much attention to this one, because my interest was more about foundation sacrifices and gargoyles, but I think it's…ah, yep. It's a demon summoning spell. Lots of details about the circles of runes you have to draw, around a bunch of candles, and something about the bait…yeah, that part's particularly gruesome. You can only summon a demon with a heart still moist with the blood of your kin." He shuddered.

Octavia forced out a smile. "That sounds really gross. Definitely not something you'd want to try at home."

"Well, no. It says you're supposed to do it on consecrated ground. Demons are dangerous."

She laughed nervously. "If you believe in

them, sure."

"I don't think they need us to believe in them to exist. But as long as you're not summoning them, I suppose you don't have any problems." Was she imagining it, or was Ben's smile knowing again? Had he overheard Tacey talking about that girls' night where they'd tried to summon demons, but gotten gargoyles instead? Maybe he had.

"Anyway…Sean Bell. What's his name doing in a demon summoning spell? Does it say?" Octavia asked.

Ben shrugged. "It's next to the part about how to cast the spell if you're after a named demon. Apparently, when you summon these things, you can just make it an open casting call, or you can mention it by name. Kind of like a call back, if you liked the first visit, and survived it, I guess. "

Wait…did that mean Sean Bell was a demon? Carline's husband, her many times great grandfather, was a freaking demon?

Not possible. Just not possible.

Wait, if Sean Bell was a demon, that meant not only was she descended from a demon, but so were Rory, Tacey, Alethea, Sybil and Callie. Callie was going to freak.

"Yeah, well, can't say I'll be doing anything like that any time soon. Or ever. Killing people and cutting out their hearts really isn't my thing." Ben offered her a smile. "But I would be interested in helping you with your history project. It sounds like fun."

"Thank you. I should probably mention that there's no payment for it, as yet. It's pretty much been just my passion project so far, but I'm hoping to make it public when I'm done. If there's any royalties out of it, I can definitely give you your fair share. Rochelle, too, if she's interested. Full credit for work done, of course. I can't even say it'll be great exposure, because I'm not sure how popular it'll be. But if you're still interested…"

Ben just laughed. "Oh, I don't need your money, Octavia. I'm doing just fine financially. Like I said, your project sounds like fun. All I ask is that if you come across anything about my Uncle Stanley Steel, you share it with me."

"Uncle Stanley?" she stammered. It wasn't possible. Like Harlow, Stan would have lived here two hundred years ago. Ben couldn't possibly be his nephew unless he was over a hundred years old, when he barely looked twenty. He probably still got asked for ID everywhere he went.

"Oh, well, that's just what I've been calling him. He disappeared almost two hundred years ago, so he can't possibly be my actual uncle. Great great great…and a few more…great uncle." He wouldn't meet her eyes, though. Like maybe he'd seen something in his research that would sound mad if he shared it, too. "Oh, but the guy you're looking for – Sean Bell. It's Callie's book, though it originally belonged to someone called Carline, so you should probably ask her more about it. I've told you all I know."

Octavia doubted that, but she also didn't know him well enough to call him on it. Tacey trusted him, which had to be enough. Whatever secrets Ben was hiding weren't her business.

"Thanks. I will."

Wow. She had another artist on board, and a history buff, to boot. Maybe her virtual world would be real sooner than she'd thought.

TWENTY-FOUR

Something was wrong, Harlow was sure of it. Octavia had barely spoken, and while she stared at the screen, her fingers weren't flying over the keyboard or the mouse like they usually did.

"What do you need my help with today?" Harlow asked.

Octavia sighed, and looked up. "I don't know if you can help. It's just…" Another sigh, deeper this time.

He moved closer to her. "Please forgive my momentary madness the other night. My actions were inexcusable. I assure you they will not happen again. I am your protector, and I will protect you, even from my own base urges."

"Base urges? Protection? Oh, shit, I was so distracted today, I forgot to buy condoms. I'm sorry. Really sorry, because another night like last night might actually be enough to forget today. Or I wish it could."

So she didn't regret being intimate with him last night? That was a relief, because he hadn't been able to stop thinking about it. About her. And about the little sounds she made when he caressed her body just right. But something was still wrong. "Did something bad happen today?"

She buried her head in her hands. "No? Yes? Actually, mostly good things have happened today. The artist I wanted to team up with for the virtual world agreed to help, and I think I might have found Sean Bell. I might have even solved the mystery of why there's no record of him until he appeared in the colony and married Carline. I'd thought the women in my family cast big shadows, but if what I've discovered today is true, his secrets are likely to overshadow us all. And I don't know what that will mean for this project, because it's hardly a normal family secret."

Harlow thought for a moment. What was the worst thing he could imagine? "Was the man a convict? Did he escape and change his name?"

Octavia laughed. "Oh, that wouldn't be a problem. Having a convict in the family is considered cool now, as long as they're long dead. No, if Sean had just been a criminal, I could have included his story alongside Carline's and thought nothing more of it. Now…I'm still trying to wrap my head around Carline having a spell book, with spells that actually worked. Like the spell that summoned you, and maybe more."

If Harlow'd had blood, it would have run cold. "Wait. Carline, the woman you think killed me, was a witch?" Actually, he'd heard rumours of such things back in Scotland, but Stan had always denied them, ready to challenge anyone for even mentioning them, that Harlow had dismissed them as the scurrilous lies Stan said they were. But if they were true…

"Yeah, I guess she was."

Wait…that wasn't the family secret that had her so upset? "What could be worse than finding out your ancestress was a witch and a killer?"

Octavia let out a nervous laugh. "When you put it like that…I guess that part didn't occur to me. I suppose we know who performed the successful summoning, then. And why she married him."

Harlow was even more confused. "You mean there are more secrets?"

"The night we summoned you, we used a spell from a book that belonged to Carline. We were supposed to be summoning a demon, not four gargoyles, which is a different spell entirely, but we were only working off Callie's translation of the original Latin, and she left out the…footnotes? Annotations? The bits that were scribbled in the margins and between the lines that weren't part of the spell. That's where I found Sean Bell's name in the original book – beside the part of the spell where you can put in the demon's name, if you're summoning one demon in particular." Octavia took a deep breath. If she were telling this to anyone except a two hundred year old gargoyle who'd actually met Carline, they'd think she was crazy. Hell, she thought she might be crazy for even thinking it. "I think Sean Bell might have been a demon. A demon Carline summoned because she wanted to marry him. Maybe he died, and the only way they could be reunited was for her to bring him back from the grave. And if she did that to him, and she had a spell for turning people into gargoyles, maybe she didn't just kill you and your family.

Maybe…maybe she's the one who turned you into what you are, and when we used her spell, or her magic, we accidentally woke you."

He was under a spell? Harlow didn't know much about magic, but he did know spells could be broken. But in order to break it, he'd need a witch, and someone who knew Latin, to better translate the spell book. Which meant he needed Grant's help, and the witch he was bound to protect.

Harlow gritted his teeth. "Then we need to find your Callie, and talk to her about this."

Octavia nodded. "She's down south for a wedding at the moment, but she should be home in a few days. As soon as I see her, I'll ask her about it."

Harlow shook his head. "Wait until I'm there with you, and I can protect you. She's a powerful witch, and she has her own gargoyle protector. She's evidently been keeping secrets from you for some time now, and who knows what she might do if you confront her. Please, promise you'll wait until dark, when I can stand beside you.”

Octavia snorted. “It’s just Callie. Sure, she’s capable of an impressive array of really nasty curses, but she’d never use one of them on her family. She’d sooner cut out her own heart than hurt one of her family!”

Carline had been family, though only a distant cousin. Grant and Stan and Wystan had been family, too, and they’d all gotten him killed. This witch had kept her powers a secret from her own family, the girls who lived under the same roof. Octavia might trust her, but Harlow wasn’t so sure.

“Please promise me,” he repeated.

“All right! I promise I won’t ask Callie anything about spells until you’re standing next to me, all hard and shirtless, to distract her. Happy?”

No, but he did feel a tiny whisper of relief. “Happy to serve and protect you, as always.”

She sighed. “Thank you. But what I really need is your help with some of these structures in Hooghly Town. You said the tavern was just a tent? I've tried to match it up with the details in the archaeological reports, but I can't seem to find evidence of anything that big. Are you sure it was here?"

Harlow took a deep breath. "Of course I'm sure. Perhaps your archaeologists simply haven't found it yet. Ah, but are you looking for a stone floor? Oh, no, the tavern floor was dirt, and it wasn't even a canvas tent so much as a hut made of branches and bark, like the native ones. The owner didn't come over on the same ships as we did. He and his wife were ex-convicts from Sydney, and it wasn't hard to see what crimes they'd been sentenced for. He bought barrels of drink, then watered it down and sold it for ten times the price to the desperate people from the *Gilmore* and the *Hooghly*. His wife was very pretty, and much younger than him, and a great favourite among the single men, for it was whispered that her favours were available for a price, as she was only his common law wife, and perhaps not even his wife at all..."

Octavia laughed. "The oldest industries in the world – drinking and sex. Nice to know they were alive and thriving, even in the early colony. Do you remember her name? Perhaps I can weave her story into the immersive, too…"

TWENTY-FIVE

It was mid afternoon when Callie's car pulled into the driveway. Octavia was eating breakfast on the veranda, making the most of the watery winter sunlight, so she lifted her hand to wave hello…only to realise that Callie wasn't alone in the car.

A strange man sat in the passenger seat, engaged in an argument with Callie.

Even stranger, she was actually arguing

back, instead of threatening to curse him, or actually putting the curse into effect.

"They were tempting me! I could not refuse their siren call!" the man insisted.

"They were cold and wrapped in plastic. Vacuum sealed. There was no way you could smell them. I get that the hot pies I bought for lunch smelled irresistible, because I couldn't wait to eat them either, but the bulk pack was supposed to be for my lunches for the next week!"

"You said I might share lunch with you. I merely took my share earlier, as I was too hungry to wait."

"Your share was not a dozen bloody pies, including the ones for next week! Admit it, Grant, you're a pie thief!"

"I have never stolen a pie in my life! You told me I could have them!"

Callie got out of the car and slammed the door. She stormed up the steps, then stopped before she reached Octavia. "That's Grant Steel. Do not trust him with pies, hot or cold, because he will inhale them like an industrial vacuum cleaner."

Grant…Steel? Harlow's brother? It couldn't be. He looked human, and he was walking in the daytime, in the sun, without turning to stone. The name was a coincidence, that was all. A descendant or distant relative…

"I can't be an industrial cleaner when I don't even know what the damn thing is!" Grant shouted as he followed Callie up the steps, then stopped when he spotted Octavia. He bowed low, like Harlow might. "My apologies, mistress. I did not see you there, or I would not have used such language. I am Grant Steel, husband to this enchanting harpy who would have me starve. Some wife you are, Calliope."

Octavia blinked. Callie had gotten married to a stranger? No way. And Callie didn't let anyone call her that.

"Callie?" she began uncertainly.

"Ignore this idiot. It was a fake engagement for my family's sake, just for the wedding."

"That's not what you said last night, wife."

Callie let huffed out an exasperated sigh. "We're not legally married under Australian law. Sure, we did what Viking traditions demanded, but we'd still have to make things official in a church or a registry office or something. And I'm not planning a wedding while there are still restrictions for this stupid virus. Look at how much trouble Kara had, planning hers. So keep a lid on that wife stuff."

"If we are not legally married, as you say, then you cannot object to me courting your pretty friend here, who might make a far more obedient wife." Grant held out his hand for Octavia's. "Pray, sweet lady, tell me your name, so that I may know how to address such an angel."

Octavia wasn't sure whether to be intrigued or horrified. He was such a terrible flirt. But she couldn't help herself. She gave him her hand, expecting a shake, but he kissed it instead.

"Mm, softer than silk. Perfection indeed.

And your name, sweet seraph?"

"This is my cousin Octavia Bell. She was there the night I summoned you, and, just like me, if you piss her off, she can unsummon you just as easily as I can. But not before I kick your arse." Callie slammed the screen door open and strode inside.

Grant bowed again. "Forgive her for her coarseness, sweet Octavia. Tell me, are you as sacrosanct as your namesake? Or are you as free with your affections as my mercurial wife?"

"Take your hands off her, Grant," came a growl from the shadows. To Octavia's surprise, Harlow emerged from the wall, in the corner where the sun did not penetrate. Unlike Grant, Harlow had wings, horns and some wicked looking claws. Her faithful, dependable stone shadow.

Grant backed up, releasing Octavia's hand as he eyed Harlow with consternation. "Brother."

Octavia blinked. "This is your sleazy

brother, and he's married to Callie?"

"He must have traded his hand in marriage for the secret to breaking the curse, for he stands in sunlight, free to move, while I must remain in the shadows. How did she do it, brother? For if she can break the spell on you, she might save us all."

Grant shrugged. "I have no idea. This morning I was a gargoyle, just like you, and I hid under a blanket in the back of Callie's car. Then she stopped for a little while, and returned with something that smelled so good, I simply couldn't help myself. I'd never been so hungry in all my life. I asked her if I might have a bite, and one was not enough. Before I knew it, I had finished all of her pies, and she had to return to the bakery for more. While I was making my way through this second batch, the blanket slid off me and exposed me to sunlight, but I barely noticed, so intent was I on my meal. It wasn't until I'd run out of pies that I realised, and Callie insisted I take the seat beside her so she might keep an eye on me." He snorted. "If I had known she would turn into such a harpy after we married, I might not have made those vows…" He sighed. "But now she is wedded and bedded, I am honour bound to make it official in the laws of this time. Alas that I did not meet the exquisite Octavia first…"

"Octavia is mine to protect, not yours," Harlow growled.

"Ladies of this time are mistresses of their own fate far more than they were in ours, brother. I'm sure Lady Octavia can make up her own mind. Would you prefer my silver tongue and smooth manners, or my brother with his coarse, untutored farmer's ways at your side?" Grant asked.

"I'll take Harlow's tongue over yours, any day or night," Octavia said, shifting into the shadows to stand with Harlow. She did not like this man. That Callie could even consider marrying him, archaic rituals aside, made no sense at all.

Grant's eyes widened. "My brother has

finally made a conquest? It is a miracle! You must allow me to tutor him in how to please a lady, mistress, before you join him in your marriage bed. Perhaps I could offer you some instruction, too…" He winked.

Octavia's blood boiled. "He pleases me just fine, you dick. Actually, I think you're the one who needs some tutoring and instruction. If you're betrothed or married or whatever to Callie, and you have any sense of self preservation, you keep it in your pants. Because if she catches you cheating on her…cursing your dick off will be just the start."

Grant took a larger step backward. "Forgive me, Lady Octavia. We are to be family, and I meant it with the utmost respect for my soon to be sister."

Harlow made a disbelieving sound in his throat.

Then Callie called from inside, "Grant? Where is that heart? I need to get it in the freezer before it goes bad. It was in the sun long enough as it was, out there on that rock. If we don't keep it fresh, the spell might not work!"

"Coming, coming." Grant grabbed a small cooler box and hurried inside with it.

TWENTY-SIX

Another car came to a halt soon after sunset, and a woman who might have been Carline returned to life climbed out. Stan appeared right behind her.

Harlow stepped back into the shadows on the veranda, so Carline or whoever she was wouldn't see him.

"Callie!" the woman shouted. "Callie, I know you're in there, because your car's here. I need to tell you something!”

The witch came running out of the house, with Grant on her heels. “Alethea? What’s wrong? What are you doing here? Is it your stalker? Have you changed your mind, and now you want me to curse him?”

“No, it’s nothing like that. It’s about…who’s he?” Alethea asked, pointing at Grant.

Grant beamed. “I am Calliope’s husband. Are you another of her lovely friends?”

“Husband?” Alethea whispered, staring at Callie.

Callie held up her hands. “I can explain.”

Harlow had to admit he was interested to hear how she’d persuaded Grant to get married.

Only another car pulled into the driveaway, with the redhead, her daughter and Wystan inside. The redhead’s eyes darted from one person to the other, taking in the situation, before shouting, “You stay here with Wystan, where you’ll be safe.” Then she climbed out of her car, her arms folded across her chest. "Who are these men, and what are they doing here?" she demanded.

The daughter tumbled out of the car, followed by Wystan. "It's all right, Mummy, they're all gargoyle monster protectors, just like Wystan! They're here to protect us!"

The redhead rounded on her daughter. "I told you to stay in the car."

"And I told her they are all my cousins, gargoyle protectors like me, who pose no danger to you or your family, who we are bound to protect," rumbled Wystan as he laid a hand on the little girl's shoulder.

"I don't care what Wystan told you. I said…"

Octavia chose that moment to walk out onto the veranda. "Oh, wow, everyone's home," she said.

The breath hissed out of the redhead. "Oh, thank God. At least one of you has some sense. You know the lease conditions. We're not supposed to have men living here, or we get tossed out."

Octavia looked around, taking in the gargoyles standing around the yard. She met Harlow's eyes briefly, before she faced the redhead. "Technically, they don't live here, and they're not entirely men, either. Well, definitely male, but they're not human. Except maybe Grant..." Her eyes turned to Callie. "I'd really like a chance to talk to you about that. And...a couple of other things, too."

Callie raised both hands in surrender. "Now we're all here, I need to talk to all of you, too. And ask for your help, so I can get some answers. How would you feel about summoning a demon again?"

"What?"

"What?"

"WHAT?"

The little girl's eyes widened. "You're going to summon another monster? Oh no, no, you have to protect us, Mr Monster!" She threw her arms around Wystan's knees and wouldn't let   go.

TWENTY-SEVEN

Several hours later, after Octavia had calmed Rory and Tacey had taken her to bed, all eight adults crowded into the lounge, where the TV took up most of one wall. The screen was dark now, for this discussion was too serious for that sort of entertainment.

"So let me get this straight," Tacey said. She pointed at Callie. "You want us to try to summon a demon again, here at Bell House, because you think you've worked out what went wrong last time and you think this time it will go right?"

Callie frowned. "Well, yes, but more than that. I want to summon a demon to answer some questions."

"So would I," Octavia chimed in, a look of determination on her face.

Alethea hesitated for a moment, then added, "Stan wants to know what happened to Carline."

Tacey waved her hands in frustration. "Does no one think this is a crazy, likely very bad idea?"

"Well, we have four gargoyle protectors, plus the four of us," Callie began. "We know Carline must have summoned a demon successfully in 1834, and she lived for decades after that. We'd only be following her instructions. With all the safeguards, we should be perfectly safe."

Octavia agreed with Callie, but she couldn't help saying, "Mostly safe. As long as we do it outside, far enough away from the house. We still don't know why the original mill burned – it might have been the demon's doing."

Callie made a noise like a spitting cat. "Or maybe Carline just knocked over a candle or a lamp one night, and that set fire to it. You don't know if the fire had anything to do with demons or magic or Carline at all."

Tacey waved at the men in the room. "What do you guys think about this? Last time we tried this spell, we brought you four back from the dead. What if, instead of a demon, we end up with more men like you?"

Grant held up his hands, his tone calm and reasonable, which automatically sent Octavia's hackles up. "I trust Callie to get the spell right this time. She has her kinsman's heart, after all, still filled with his blood. The chances of there being more gargoyles like us here are very low. I mean, this is your home, not a cemetery. Who'd be buried here?"

Octavia opened her mouth to mention the Hooghly Town cemetery, near the southern edge of the property, where the regional park began. Harlow had said he'd felt something there the night he disappeared, though he hadn't been sure what. There might be more gargoyles, or all kinds of things they didn't know about.

Grant continued, "So when Callie summons this demon…"

"Sean Bell. His name is Sean Bell," Octavia piped up.

Grant inclined his head. "So when Callie summons this demon, Sean Bell, he will be under her control, and she can ask all of your questions. We'll all be here to help in case anything goes wrong, and four gargoyles against one demon are not good odds for the demon, even if he could escape Callie's safeguards, which I doubt, because my wife is nothing if not an incredibly powerful witch." He gave Callie such a besotted look that Octavia almost laughed.

"Lovesick fool," Harlow whispered, half under his breath.

Octavia was inclined to agree, but she wanted this as much as Callie did. The only way to truly know Sean Bell's story was to ask him, and if he answered a demon summoning spell, then she already had the most important answer of all. Of course, that would also mean that they were all descended from the marriage of a demon and a witch, but she didn't dare mention that yet. Not until she was certain.

"We will protect you. Nothing will happen to any of you ladies. I swear it," Wystan said.

Stan rose. "I, too, will swear it."

Grant rolled his eyes. "Of course it won't. This is perfectly safe!"

Harlow blew out a breath. They were back at the mill all over again, about to follow Grant in doing the most stupid thing he could possibly think of. "This time, when something goes wrong, I will be here to save you." But his eyes weren't on Grant. Instead, he was staring at Octavia.

Octavia's mouth went dry. She understood, and nodded.

Callie rubbed her hands together. "All right, let's do this!"

TWENTY-EIGHT

This time, the ritual seemed to proceed so much faster. Maybe it was because Callie had marked the circles of runes before, or that there was almost no wind down in the dip of the driveway between Bell House and the ruins of Bell Cottage. Maybe it was because they weren't trespassing on the site of a centuries old cemetery, but instead performing the ritual on their own property. When Octavia had mentioned the need for consecrated ground, Callie had produced a big bottle of holy water and blessed the site herself, insisting she was better at this than most priests, plus she pronounced the Latin words right.

Octavia wasn't sure, but it seemed almost no time at all before she was holding hands with Wystan and Harlow, part of a circle that included all the Bell House girls except Rory, and all four gargoyles. If Grant was still a gargoyle – she still wasn't sure about that, and Callie had been too busy preparing the spell to give her answers.

Oh, well. Hopefully when Sean Bell arrived in the centre of the circle, he'd have all the answers she needed.

At Callie's nod, the chanting began.

"We command thee, Sean Bell, demon, to enter this circle. You will help protect us, obey our commands, and answer our questions, as long as you are under our command, or within this circle…"

Just like the first time, Octavia felt the

power rising up from their circle, tingling in her hands. Almost like magic, the heart in the centre of the salt circle began to glow.

"We command thee, Sean Bell, demon, to enter this circle…"

Wind rose up, whipping at their hair and clothes, but it didn't touch the candles in the centre of their circle. Now the power was humming through her. Octavia could barely believe it, but this time she had no doubts. The spell had worked before, and it would work now, too. It was already working. She could feel it.

"What in the devil's name are you doing? Stop that at once!" an unfamiliar male voice roared.

The chanting faltered, then resumed, louder than ever.

"I said stop that! Do you want to set off the wards? If you open a portal to hell on the property, you'll wake everything, and let me tell you, demons will be the least of your problems then!" the voice threatened.

Octavia looked around. Storming down the driveway, as though he'd come from Bell House, was a man built like a wrestler. For a moment, she thought he had wings like Harlow, but then she blinked and realised he was just bulky – muscles upon muscles that made all the gargoyles look slim by comparison.

But the others hadn't stopped chanting. If anything, they'd only gotten louder, to drown out the intruder's voice.

"For the last time, stop that before I set fire to something!" the man roared. He shoved between Octavia and Wystan, breaking their joined hands, and grabbed the glowing heart from the centre of the salt circle. He held it up in one meaty fist and squashed it to a pulp, then threw it into the bush. "Now, which of you came up with this stupid scheme?"

They all looked at each other. The idea had been Callie's, for it had been her spell book, but they owed this stranger nothing.

Callie stepped forward, chin jutting toward

the stranger as her eyes flashed. "Who the fuck are you, and what are you doing on our property? You'd better have a good answer for me, or I'll curse you so completely you'll wish we'd opened a portal and shoved you through it."

The man snorted. "You've never seen hell, Calliope, and none of you would survive a day there."

Callie's hands balled into fists. "Last chance, arsehole. Name, and what you're doing here, before we throw you the fuck off our property and call the police."

Wings popped out of the man's back, bigger than Harlow's, as horns sprouted from his head and he took a distinctly reddish cast.

"I'm Sean Bell, and this is my property, and has been since the day the Governor gave it to me," the demon growled.

TWENTY-NINE

They went from chanting to swearing in a moment, as even Callie looked pale at the demon standing outside all her protective bespelled circles. But no one was game to run. Besides, where would they run to? They were home, and this demon, if he really was Sean Bell, had to know this place as well as they did. He'd owned it since he'd married Carline Steel.

A crazy idea came to Octavia, along with

courage she had not known she possessed. "You won't hurt us, because we're your great-great-great granddaughters. You invited us here, to live in Bell House, to keep us safe. Carline summoned you the night the mill burned, didn't she, and you married her."

The demon blinked at her. "Which one are you?"

"Octavia Bell," she answered, then added, "Sir." It seemed sensible to be at least a little respectful. He was her ancestor, after all.

He nodded. "The younger sister. The maiden, not the mother."

Octavia felt her cheeks grow hot. If that bloody burglar hadn't stolen her condoms, she'd have done the deed with Harlow, and she wouldn't be a virgin any more.

"Was this your idea, young maiden?" Sean asked, waving at the circle.

"I just wanted answers," Octavia said.

A delighted grin appeared on the demon's face. "Oh, that's precious! You wanted to summon a demon just to talk? When you could have asked for anything? You're even more of an innocent than my Carline was!" He rubbed his hands together. "Well, seeing as you're the first of my descendants to actually discover the truth on your own, I suppose it would be nice to have a proper conversation, without having to hide anything. I don't suppose you have anything to drink in this house of yours, hmm? Temperance was a terrible thing, when it was in vogue…"

Octavia wasn't sure how it happened. One minute, they were standing outside, staring at a demon, and the next, they were sitting in the lounge room with cider bottles in hand, with a man who wouldn't have looked out of place in public, not a wing or horn to be seen. The same couldn't be said about the three gargoyles, though. Wystan, Harlow and Stan all had their horns out, bristling if Sean so much as looked their way.

Grant, on the other hand, looked as human as Sean, with a lazy smile on his face as he held Callie on his lap. Even stranger was that Callie stayed there.

"So, which ones are you? Carline made so many gargoyles, mostly when I was away from home, so I didn't keep track of all of them."

"Grant, Harlow, Wystan and Stanley Steel," Grant drawled, pointing at each man in turn.

Sean's eyes widened. "Oh, you were her first! She never was sure whether the spell had been successful, seeing as bloody William never did tell her where he'd buried your bodies. I don't suppose you'll tell me? Carline had her suspicions, of course…"

"East Perth Cemeteries," Alethea said softly. "But on the edge of one of the more recent burial grounds, with buildings on top of the graves. Almost like someone had wanted to give the bodies a decent burial, but didn't want them to be found."

Sean nodded. "Ah, that sounds like William. Always trying to protect Carline, even if he hadn't the slightest idea how to do it. If he'd buried you at the mill like she'd wanted, she'd never have been in danger, and I wouldn't have had to save her. She and I might never have…well. But I'd like to think that destiny brought us together." He turned to Octavia. "So, how did you find them, to summon them?"

Callie was the one who answered, "I found Carline's spell book, and we went to the cemetery to summon a demon. We only had a pig's heart, and we got interrupted then just like we did tonight, so we never completed the spell. I think it was a combination of the incantation calling for the demon's help, and the urgency when the security guard appeared, that woke the foundation sacrifices," Callie said. "You guys, I mean."

Harlow leaned forward. "How did you break the curse on Grant? Turn him from gargoyle to human again?"

Callie eyed Grant. "I'd like to think it was him gorging himself on my pies, but I don't think that's what it was. The book says that to break the curse, you have to melt a heart of stone. A friend told me it's not so much literal melting as a metaphorical thing. The protector has to become more fully himself, to willingly choose the path fate would have had him walk if he had never been cursed."

Grant slapped his thigh. "See? I told you! It was all the sex. Fate wanted me to seduce you, then marry you, so that you would feed me as many pies as I could stomach. We did all that and more!"

Octavia had never seen Callie blush before. Callie didn't blush ever.

"I still think killing my uncle might have had something to do with it. I mean, you did help me cut out his heart," Callie muttered.

Wait…the heart Callie had put in the circle this time hadn't been a pig's heart? She'd killed someone for it?

"Callie…" Tacey began.

"Oh, don't get your knickers in a twist. He had it coming, and it was an accident that was totally his fault. I would have liked to kill him, and I could say that I helped, but if he hadn't suddenly gotten all slippery, maybe he wouldn't have died." Grant shrugged. "It was no great loss."

Callie held up her hands. "I wasn't even there. My uncle went fishing on the rocks, and his corpse washed up a day later. Rogue waves wash people off the rocks there all the time. There are warning signs everywhere, but they still do it. It could have been an accident."

Nobody believed it, though.

Not even Sean, who chuckled. "You're definitely Carline's descendant. In front of everyone, she'd deny ever meeting a man she'd killed, but afterwards…she'd sometimes feel a little regret. I'd remind her that they'd set off her wards, by coming onto the property with the intention to harm her, and they deserved their fate. Eventually, she forgot about them. All except you four. Maybe because you were family."

To Octavia's surprise, Sean was looking at the men, and not any of the girls. "What do you mean they were family?" she asked.

"William Steel and Carline were descended

from the baron's oldest son from his first marriage, the one who inherited everything. The rest of us were from younger sons, from his second marriage. We all bore the same name, yet they were nobility, and the rest of us were commoners, so far beneath them William once threatened to kill me for daring to even look at his sister," Stan said. "I never thought she'd be the one to kill me instead."

Sean looked sad. "She regretted it, right up until the end. Wanted me to keep looking for your bodies, even if William had taken that secret to his own grave, years before. She asked me to hold your things in trust, too. At first, it was a blessing, going down to Murray River alone, seeing to the farm and the cottage and resetting the wards, before returning to Bell Cottage to take care of the rest of our family. Now, it's more of a chore, flying over the new development out there, where your lands are the only farms left."

All four gargoyles leaned forward as one. "We still have our land grants?" Harlow blurted out.

"I've held them in trust since Carline first found out about them. William wanted them, you see, and she wouldn't let him have them. They were yours, and I was to return them to you if you ever rose again. You were her first foundation sacrifices, so she never was sure if she'd done the spell properly, but she said it was just in case. I can have my lawyer draw up the transfer documents – at my cost, of course – to have your lands handed back to you. I should warn you, there are some land developers down that way that would sell their souls for your property. The last offer was upward of twenty million dollars…and that was just for one block, mind. They weren't mine to sell, so I could not take any of the offers, but they're yours to do what you wish with. Even if you wish to return to farming them – the choice is yours."

"What about the cottage? Is it still there?" Harlow asked.

Sean nodded. "Just as you left it. The wards

there are strongest, as they're for more than just protection. There's a powerful spell to keep people away from the cottage, fuelled by demon blood, of course. I usually slept a night there after renewing them to recover. But no one else has been inside since you left, I promise you."

"Built before the Round House in Fremantle was completed. Does that make my cottage the oldest building still standing in Western Australia?" Harlow asked.

Octavia's heart stopped. "What?" she breathed.

Harlow grinned. "I can't show you the tent we lived in at Hooghly Town, but I can show you the stone cottage we built later that year, down by the Murray River. You might want to bring your camera, as I think this might help with your virtual world."

"When can we go?" Octavia asked. "Now?"

Sean cleared his throat. "Don't hesitate on my account. That place has been waiting a long time for human habitation. I'll be in contact as needed, while we put the paperwork through. Of course, if you ladies have taken up with these men, I won't be renewing your lease when the term ends. Carline was adamant that this house was to provide a home to girls who needed a place to stay, where they might be free from the menfolk who wanted to control their lives. Seems to me, you're all mistresses of your own destiny now, and as these boys are all millionaires, or they will be once the paperwork's sorted, you'll be well provided for, one way or another. Come next year, Bell House will be home to new girls who need a fresh start."

"Wait!" Stan said, holding up his hand. "Before you go…I need to know one thing. Is Carline in hell for what she did?"

Sean turned dark eyes on the gargoyle, like he was reading his soul. For all that he looked human, he was very much a demon in that moment. "You're the one who wanted to steal her, aren't you?"

Stan nodded. "It's a fine Scottish tradition,

going back centuries…"

"Oh, there are all sorts of traditions that go back millennia, far more stupid than that one. I could tell you stories…" Sean began, then turned serious again. "Are you fool enough to believe a woman deserves eternal damnation for defending herself against a stranger who tries to kidnap her? She didn't even know your name before she'd killed you, lad. I would have done it for her, and happily. Carline deserves happiness, though she feared hell as much as any normal god-fearing woman. It was killing you boys that made her think she might go there, and why she showed me how to perform a foundation sacrifice. She'd rather be a gargoyle like you than a demon like me, and I've always been obedient to her wishes. I'm her demon, after all."

Octavia's mouth dropped open. "You mean Carline's still alive?"

Sean winked. "Smart girl, this one. I suspect you get that from me, or maybe my father."

Demons had fathers?

He must have read the question in his eyes, for Sean just shrugged and said, "Lucifer. Not that he was ever around much. Probably doesn't even remember me. No matter, though, I have my life here, and now I no longer have a cottage to keep, I'll have time to find some new tenants for when you move out. Weren't you going, girl?"

Octavia had a hundred more questions, but she was too flustered to decide which one to ask next, so she allowed Harlow to pull her out of the room, to where her car waited.

"Your camera gear is still in the back. We can drive down most of the way, and I'll fly you in from the river," Harlow said.

The oldest building in Western Australia. A cottage built by Harlow and his family, before anything else she'd ever seen. Left exactly as it had been built, in 1834…

Who cared about demons when she had history to discover?

"Let's go," Octavia said.

THIRTY

"It's perfect," Octavia breathed as she stepped out of the cottage. "It really is exactly as you left it. Clothes, tools…"

"Except for the black rocks around the property line. Those were white in my time," Harlow said.

"He did say something about demon blood wards…" Octavia reminded him.

"Yes, but blood is red, fading to rust, or

brown. Not black…"

"Maybe demon blood is black. Or he mixed it with something. I wouldn't know the first thing about spells. Of the two I've tried to help Callie cast, neither of them actually worked, so your guess is probably as good as mine. Not that I care about spells. I'm in love with this cottage. I want to come back here during the day and photograph everything. And I want to take pictures of you wearing your old clothes from back then, too. Oh, that would be perfect…" Octavia's tongue couldn't keep up with her thoughts, they came so fast. Harlow's cottage – for he'd told her they'd built it on his land, intending to build houses for the others when they returned, which they never did – was like a dream come true.

"We could come and live here, if you like. Me and my farm…we're all yours, if you'll have us."

In the dark, she couldn't see his expression, but she knew his eyes were on her.

"Was that…did you just propose marriage,

Mr Steel?"

He ducked his head. "I suppose I did. I can't imagine spending the rest of my life with anyone else, and the moment I'm alone with you, I start thinking about doing things only married people are supposed to do, so I figured…"

"The oldest building in the state still standing on twenty million dollars' worth of land, and a lifetime with the one man I'd like to do things only married people are supposed to do? What girl could refuse an offer like that?"

She couldn't say no. Not to Harlow, even though she hadn't known him long.

"You're not accepting it, either," he said.

Octavia closed her eyes. "Ask me again when I've finished the immersive. The whole point of making it is to make me feel brave, more like the other women in my family instead of just a shadow who's never done anything on her own. Never accomplished anything. When I've done it, when it's released to the public so people can know Carline's story and yours…well, as much as we're willing to tell people…then I think I might be just brave enough to take the next step."

Harlow bowed his head. "Then it is a good thing I did not make love to you the other night, or you might have felt forced into a marriage before you are ready. Waiting will be hard, but I know it will be worth it. All the more reason to help you finish your project, as the sooner it is done, the sooner you might be ready to consider doing…other things."

Octavia couldn't help it. She laughed. "Oh, I might not be ready to marry you, but I'm definitely ready for sex. In fact…everyone's at Bell House tonight. There'll be no one in the café, and I have a bed…"

"Are you sure?"

"Positive."

THIRTY-ONE

In the studio, they found a big box of condoms on the bed with a note from Rochelle and Ben. "Have fun," was all it said.

Harlow had Octavia wet, naked and begging for more before she could think, and then she couldn't think, for he was there between her thighs, hot and hard and wearing a condom that looked like it had ridges down its length. A lot like the vibrator in her bottom drawer.

Not to mention an extra bulge near the base that looked like…

The knowing look in his eyes told her everything. He'd watched every moment that night, when she thought she'd been alone. If only he'd joined her in bed then…

The head of his cock was hotter and harder than any machine. Bigger, too, but she wasn't afraid of that now. This was Harlow, and she wanted everything he could give her.

"Are you sure?" he asked again, stroking her clit.

God, she was going to come again if he kept that up. And she didn't want to until he was buried deep inside her, all the way.

"Yes. Please!" she begged.

With one long, slow thrust that seemed to go on forever, he entered her.

Octavia held her breath, moaning as each ridge bumped along inside her, stretching her beyond anything she'd ever felt before. So full, and still he kept coming, until she felt the extra bulge bump her clit.

"Are you all right?" he asked, shifting a little so that bulge rubbed her clit just right.

"I'm…I'm…" Then she detonated, so all she could see was stars.

Somewhere far away, she heard Harlow say, "My God, Octavia, that feels…like heaven. I want to stay buried this deep in you forever."

And then he began to move, those ridges rubbing all the right places so she could scarcely think. She could hear her voice chanting yes, yes, yes, in between begging for more, until he gave it to her. Pounding into her harder than the waves on the breakwater, as orgasms flew thick and fast. She scarcely had the breath to scream between one and the next, but she didn't care, for Harlow was everything she'd ever wanted, and she only wished this night might never end.

THIRTY-TWO

The afternoon light streamed through Octavia's window, waking Harlow from sleep. He always woke before her, but he had only to slip a finger between her thighs and she was awake and ready for him. Last night, she'd finally agreed to marry him, and his mind was still filled with joy at the thought.

Joy and more than a little madness, for he stuck his hand in the sun. He expected to see it turn to stone, but this time, it didn't change. Somehow, he'd broken the curse. Just like Grant.

He made leisurely love to Octavia before they both rose and dressed. Tonight, all of her housemates were home, and she'd promised to show them her work. The first stage of her virtual world was finished, and starting next week, it would be released to the public.

Grant was already in the lounge room, with Callie sitting in his lap.

Rory was lying on the rug, her drawings and pencils spread out across half the floor. Tacey was in the kitchen, preparing snacks to go with the presentation, or at least that's what she'd said. Alethea and Stan had claimed one of the couches, so Harlow perched on the end.

Someone knocked on the door, and Octavia went to answer it. Rochelle and Ben — their party was complete.

Wystan and Tacey came out of the kitchen, carrying huge trays of food that took up the whole coffee table.

Harlow inhaled. Oh, he wanted to eat everything, and from the look on Grant's face, he felt the same.

First, he had to be polite and watch what Octavia wanted to show them. She'd worked so hard at it, it was only fair.

"All right, now we're all here…" Octavia pressed a button, and the screen filled with *Shadows of the Swan*, the name she'd given her world. "This is Fremantle, as the first settlers found it…"

Fremantle and Hooghly Town and the Mill. She'd release with only the three places to start with, and add his Murray River farm as an expansion after release, she'd said. She'd decided to turn it into a sort of game, where you could choose which settler's path to follow, and then you had to survive in the early colony – no easy feat, he knew.

The pictures on the screen brought tears to his eyes, they were so lifelike. That was Octavia and Ben's work, he knew, taking his descriptions and a mysterious sketchbook full of pictures from 1850s Fremantle that had appeared one day, to turn the world he remembered into reality once more.

When Octavia was done, they all clapped. Now she was the one who had tears in her eyes.

"So many people have signed up to be notified even before it goes live on Kickstarter. Hundreds of them! I can't believe it," Octavia said.

Rochelle glanced at Ben. They'd been instrumental in helping with the social media campaign, whatever that meant. All Harlow understood was that a lot of people liked Ben's art and when he'd told them he'd helped create the game, they'd all signed up overnight.

"It makes me wish we'd actually gotten to live there, instead of selling the land," Grant said. He, Wystan and Stan had made agreements with developers to build houses on their farms. Harlow had sold a little of his land, but he'd kept the half with the cottage, at Octavia's insistence. She'd made him promise they could spend their honeymoon in the cottage, and even if he wasn't a gargoyle any more, he still couldn't refuse.

Not that he wanted to. Taking her home to the cottage seemed…fitting, somehow. He couldn't change the past but he liked the future they were shaping together.

A future they'd never have had if Grant hadn't decide to raid the mill that fateful night in 1834.

"If we'd never raided the mill, we wouldn't be here now, with these wonderful women," Harlow said. "We'd have lived and died on those farms, and never known what might have been."

Grant looked at him strangely. "You almost sound like you think one of my crazy schemes was actually a good thing."

"Maybe it was. Even if I couldn't see it at the time, because raiding the mill still was a stupid thing to do, but it turned out all right in the end," Harlow said. "Besides, I need a man to stand witness at our wedding, and I believe that's traditionally a role for a man's brother."

Grant's eyes widened. "You're getting married? I don't believe it! You hear that, Callie? There's going to be a wedding! Want to make ours official, and make it a double?"

The sound of a ringing phone drowned out Callie's response.

Tacey frowned. "It looks like an international number."

"Probably some scammer, trying to get your bank details. Just ignore it," Octavia advised.

But Tacey had already hit the green button. "Hello?"

"Tacey? Is that you? It's Sybil!"

The girls all exclaimed at hearing her voice.

"Who's there?" Sybil asked.

Tacey grinned. "I have you on speaker, because I'm home with Rory, Octavia, Alethea, Callie and Rochelle." She didn't mention the men.

"Oh, perfect! So I can tell all of you – I met someone up here, a real Viking, so I'm staying for another season so we can work on this dig together. We've already found so much, but we're hoping for an ice mummy, like Otzi. Seeing as the borders are still closed, it's probably the best place for me, until it's safe to come home. We're pretty isolated, so we've missed the worst of the pandemic in the big cities so far. Even now I'm in civilisation, it's a tiny little town, and half of it's taken up by our research labs. Can you believe there's still snow on the ground in summer?"

"It was like that in Scotland sometimes," someone said, and Harlow felt himself nodding.

"Who was that? Who else is there? Has one of you finally gotten a boyfriend?" Sybil demanded.

"Well, Octavia's engaged, and her and Callie are considering a double wedding when the weather gets warmer and the restrictions ease," Tacey said.

"What? Oh, I want to be there. Callie and Octavia getting married? And here I thought you or Alethea would be first..."

Alethea leaned forward. "What about you? Did you say you'd met someone in the Arctic? Is he hot?"

Tacey aimed a half-hearted kick at Alethea.

"Didn't I tell you? Oh, you have to meet Thor. He's a real, live Viking, just like they made them a thousand years ago. I'd take him over a Hemsworth any day, because he's the real deal. Oh, did you say Callie's there?"

"I'm here!" Callie called, reaching for a muffin and waving it like a flag, even though Sybil couldn't see her.

"Hey, in all your research on ancient spells and stuff, did you ever run into mentions about foundation sacrifices, or gargoyles?" Sybil asked.

The whole room fell silent.

Even Callie didn't seem sure how to answer that one.

"Oh, wait, I've just got an emergency message coming through…we were supposed to ship out in a week, with the next donkey supply run, but they've found something in the glacier that needs to be helicoptered to the lab right away, which means I need to get out to the helipad if I want a ride. It might be a body buried in the ice - a real live Viking!" She ended the call without even saying goodbye.

Callie looked worried. "Did she really say gargoyles and foundation sacrifices?"

"And a real, live Viking, buried in the ice?" Octavia asked. "Shouldn't she mean a dead one, if he's been there for a thousand years?"

Ben grinned. "Sounds like she might have found another one of us!"

"Surely not…" But even as the words left Alethea's lips, no one believed them.

ABOUT THE AUTHOR

Demelza Carlton has always loved the ocean, but on her first snorkelling trip she found she was afraid of fish.

She has since swum with sea lions, sharks and sea cucumbers and stood on spray drenched cliffs over a seething sea as a seven-metre cyclonic swell surged in, shattering a shipwreck below.

Demelza now lives in Perth, Western Australia, the shark attack capital of the world.

The *Ocean's Gift* series was her first foray into fiction, followed by her suspense thriller *Nightmares* trilogy. She swears the *Mel Goes to Hell* series ambushed her on a crowded train and wouldn't leave her alone.

Want to know more? You can follow Demelza on Facebook, Twitter, YouTube or her website, Demelza Carlton's Place at:

www.demelzacarlton.com

More Books by Demelza Carlton

<u>**Colony: Aqua series**</u>

Halcyon (#1)

Poseidon (#2)

Apollo (#3)

<u>**Colony: Nyx series**</u>

Fang (#1)

Talon (#2)

Claw (#3)

<u>**Siren of Secrets series**</u>

Ocean's Secret (#1)

Ocean's Gift (#2)

Ocean's Infiltrator (#3)

<u>**Nightmares Trilogy**</u>

Nightmares of Caitlin Lockyer (#1)

Necessary Evil of Nathan Miller (#2)

Afterlife of Alana Miller (#3)

<u>**Mel Goes to Hell series**</u>

The Devil's Work (#1)

See You in Hell (#2)

Mel Goes to Hell (#3)

To Hell and Back (#4)

The Holiday From Hell (#5)

All Hell Breaks Loose (#6)

The Devil Goes to Heaven (#7)

<u>**Romance Island Resort series**</u>

Maid for the Rock Star (#1)

The Rock Star's Email Order Bride (#2)

The Rock Star's Virginity (#3)

The Rock Star and the Billionaire (#4)

The Rock Star Wants A Wife (#5)

The Rock Star's Wedding (#6)

Maid for the South Pole (#7)

Romance a Medieval Fairytale series

Enchant: Beauty and the Beast Retold

Dance: Cinderella Retold

Fly: Goose Girl Retold

Revel: Twelve Dancing Princesses
Retold

Silence: Little Mermaid Retold

Awaken: Sleeping Beauty Retold

Embellish: Brave Little Tailor Retold

Appease: Princess and the Pea Retold

Blow: Three Little Pigs Retold

Return: Hansel and Gretel Retold

Wish: Aladdin Retold

Melt: Snow Queen Retold

Spin: Rumpelstiltskin Retold

Kiss: Frog Prince Retold

Reflect: Snow White Retold

Roar: Goldilocks Retold

Cobble: Elves and the Shoemaker Retold

Float: Enchanted Horse Retold

Steal: Forty Thieves Retold

Call: Pied Piper Retold

Fall: Scheherazade Retold

Feather: Swan Maidens Retold

Cross: Billy Goats Gruff Retold

Weave: Rapunzel Retold

Claim: Puss in Boots Retold

Curse: Rose Red Retold

Cross: Three Billy Goats Gruff Retold

Weave: Rapunzel Retold

Claim: Puss in Boots Retold

<u>**Heart of Steel series**</u>

Heart of Steel (#0)

Stone Guardian (#1)

Stone Champion (#2)

Stone Sentinel (#3)

Stone Shadow (#4)

www.ingramcontent.com/pod-product-compliance
Lightning Source LLC
Chambersburg PA
CBHW070620170726

48291CB00003B/807